ADRIAN-ORION'S BELT

By

S. A. GEORGE

ADRIAN-ORION'S BELT

iUniverse books may be ordered through booksellers or by contacting:

iUniverse
1663 Liberty Drive
Bloomington, IN 47403
www.iuniverse.com
1-800-Authors (1-800-288-4677)

ISBN: 978-1-5320-1371-3 (sc)
ISBN: 978-1-5320-1372-0 (e)

Print information available on the last page.

iUniverse rev. date: 03/13/2017

DEDICATIONS

Mankind has enjoyed viewing the stars since creation – reaching out into a vast universe, unlocking the secrets in store, out there somewhere; we see His handiwork.

To Ida and Rodger for being very supportive and encouraging. Rodger was a Sergeant and was a part of the Normandy Beach Invasion, Omaha, in World War II.

To the U.S. Army. Thank you for your sacrifice preserving our freedoms here and aboard.

To Kay, thank you for this collaboration, five books, several years, a best friend, and typing these manuscripts.

Thank you Master Sergeant Dean Welch, Army Public Affairs in New York for explaining several terms associated with the Army. We appreciate your service as well in the military.

This is a team of Airborne Rangers forming a Special Ops, some coming from other countries.

- **LT. COLONEL DAVID EISEN:**
  Commander of Special Ops Team, Orion's Belt; Mission Planning Specialist, TA to Professor Baldwin and later Professor Rodgers, both Astrophysicists. Colonel Eisen graduated from USC in Los Angeles with a degree in Astrophysics; joined the Airborne Army Rangers. Alias Gerald Wayne.

- **PROFESSOR ADRIAN RODGERS:**
  Called Mafusa, Vegan extraterrestrial; taught Astrophysics, replaced Professor Baldwin.

- **PROFESSOR BALDWIN:**
  David Eisen's Professor of Astrophysics at USC in Los Angeles.

- **MAJOR OALOFF:**
  Orion's Belt – Norwegian - Could fix identity changes as well as Biometrics Analysis; seasoned Mission Specialist, Army.

- **FIRST LIEUTENANT PETTIGREW:**
  Survivalist, Tracking, Grenadier, Army, could fix tactical vehicles, motors - Orion's Belt.

- **SERGEANT VINNIE PARTER:**
  Demolitions, Grenadier, Orion's Belt – Army.

- **COMMAND SERGEANT PREACHER JOHN CHURCH:**
Ex-Preacher, best of the snipers, tries to be a morale booster as he quotes verses in the Bible and not in the Bible; Army, Texan, Orion's Belt.

- **SECOND LIEUTENANT SUNRISE:**
Ethiopian Military - Can fly anything; back ground as a mechanic, Navy. Joined Orion's Belt.

- **SERGEANT IVAN ROMANOFF:**
Member of the CPT (Cyber Protection Team), computer genius, tracking network; Russian military, Army, Orion's Belt.

- **PRIVATE SCHWARTZ KLINE:**
Sniper, can fix any weapon, Army; Orion's Belt.

- **CAPTAIN CHAN HO:**
Drone Specialist, Gunner, small sword and weapon skills; Orion's Belt.

- **GENERAL STEVENS:**
Commander of Army Base at Los Alamitos. Now known as the Joint Forces Training Base. Gave Orion's Belt their orders. Became a surrogate father to David Eisen when his parents died suddenly; Wife is Nancy.

- **COLONEL BLAKE BARNARD:**
Mission Coordinator Assisting David and the General.

- **VICKIE AMIMOUR:**
Archaeologist-Assistant to Dr. Maleke; works to recover art and ancient relics and prosecute those who steal or destroy artifacts.

- **DR. ANA CORDIERO:**
British; Therapist on base helping soldiers psychologically. Love interest of David.

- **MIKE:**
  David's younger nephew.

- **STEIL:**
  Name of Private Bentley's nemesis.

- **DIPLOMAT SELBY:**
  David accompanied him to several regions to talk with world leaders and encourage them to help American Defense Forces fighting with them against Nibus.

- **CHUL-MOO:**
  President-Dictator of North Korea – Name means 'Weapon of Iron'.

- **NIBUS:**
  An all encompassing name for a Middle Eastern Radical Terrorist Group.

- **BARREL BOMB:**
  As used against Syrian civilians, is an improvised unguided bomb (a flying IED) filled with shrapnel, oil or chemicals (explosive).

- **THE EXPLORER:**
  Carlile Ironstone's 300-foot submarine dedicated to improving the oceans.

- **JAMS RATCLIFF:**
  Director of Recoveries at the Art Loss Register in England.

- **DR. MALEKE:**
  The Curator of the Education Heritage Museum in Aleppo Province.

- **COLONEL COSTANZA GOODING:**
  Commander of Orion's Belt until retiring. Recruited David; Army.

- **BEN:**
Substitute for David as TA.

- **COLONEL MINH:**
North Vietnam Commander of a few soldiers embedded in the jungle who were basically mercenaries paid by frightened citizens, farmers and the like to protect them from raiders who would destroy their farms. They had no dealings with the Government other than to watch for activity where the old border between North and South was; now all one country, Communist.

- **LIEUTANT MAO:**
Ruthless soldier under Colonel Minh's command.

- **REX:**
David's dog, served on several missions; Army.

- **KYLE:**
Worked at Griffin's Electronics (part owner).

- **SCOTT:**
Radicalized 'Lone Wolf' to terrorism.

- **MINDY:**
Model at Dellas – girlfriend to Scott.

- **GENERAL GONZALES:**
Ruthless drug lord in Peru, friend of Colonel Eisen.

- **SHELIAH:**
David's love interest in Peru – she was allied with and fought for General Gonzales.

- **CARLILE IRONSTONE:**
Entrepreneur, Ocean Conservationist, helped funding for students' education, especially those joining various Think Tanks.

- **DEAN ATWELL:**

Dean at USC, where David got his degree; Professor Baldwin and Professor Adrian Rodgers taught there.

- **DANIELS:**
Friend of David's – surveillance.

- **REESE:**
Molecular Biologist – specialized in DNA

- **THINK TANK:**
Established to bring ideas for conservation and stopping pollution.

- **NORA:**
Private Bentley's wife (Amish).

- **PRIVATE AL BENTLEY:**
Will Hutchins; Army, Radio Base Operator.

- **SPECIAL OPS:**
Special Operations, Army and other military forces.

- **CECILY:**
David's Sister

- **GRANT:**
David's brother-in-law.

- **MAJOR YOUSSUF MOHAMMAD:**
Ex-follower of Radical Islam Leader named Warrior. Expert on mission planning and interrogating terrorists.

- **GENET:**
Love interest of Major Youssuf Mohammad. Liberian Nurse, captive of Radical Islam leader Warrior.

- **THE JOINT FORCES TRAINING BASE:**
In Los Alamitos, California – where Colonel Eisen got his training as an Airborne Ranger.

- **TAYLOR:**

Think Tank recruit who followed Adrian.

- **SETH:**
  Think Tank recruit who disagreed with Adrian's plans.

- **LE MUR:**
  Terrorist, pipeline drug lord posing as a legitimate business man, resides in three countries; French (his name means 'The Wall').

- **AIRBORNE RANGERS:**
  Report to the Joint Special Operations Command (JSOC).

- **DR. GRIFFO:**
  One of Adrian's students. A Think Tank recruit in charge of the Phoenix Computer, the most sophisticated in the world.

- **CHARLOTTE:**
  Oaloff's girlfriend, later his wife.

- **AMR al-AZM:**
  Archaeologist in Middle East.

- **DR. COOK:**
  Director of Ancient Relics in the Middle East.

- **DR. O'KEEFE:**
  Physicist, expert on bombs.

- **MAYLA IBRÂHÎM:**
  Radical Jihadist.

- **ABDESLAM:**
  Brother of Mayla

- **AGENT SCOTT:**
  With FBI.

- **AGENTS WELLS AND BURK:**
  Department of Homeland Security

- **HOTAK SIKANDER KAHN:**
  An Afghan helping the Americans giving intel on the Taliban.

- **PROFESSOR STEPHEN W. HAWKING:**
  Author of 'A Brief History of Time'. Formerly the Lucasian professor of mathematics at Cambridge University considered the most brilliant theoretical physicist since Einstein. An imaginary visit with Professor Hawking is in this book.

- **BASHAR al-ASAD:**
  President – Dictator of Syria

- **KLICK:**
  1000 meters, a distance of one kilometer or .62 miles.

- **TIC:**
  Troops in Contact with the enemy.

- **CPT:**
  Cyber Protection Teams – a significant step in boosting State and Federal cyber defense capabilities – CPTs will be stationed around the US and will be staffed mainly by National Guard Citizen-Soldiers.

- **IED:**
  Improvised Explosive Device

- **MORTER:**
  Short-barreled cannon.

- **DMZ:**
  Demilitarized Zone.

- **BRITISH 717:**
  Only weapon not developed as mentioned in this book.

- **CH-47 D:**
  Chinook helicopter; twin engine, tandem rotors, heavy-lift helicopter, 196 MPH top speed, carries 33 – 55 troops. Can handle two large underslung containers.

- **BLACKHAWK-UH 60:**
  Single rotor, 14 troops, can carry cargo as vehicles in sling load. Twin engine, the army's primary medium lift utility transport and air assault aircraft – the UH-60L Blackhawk is an upgrade. The HH-Pave Hawk is a derivative of the UH-60 Blackhawk.

- **TATP:**
  An explosive easily made by terrorists and usually concealed in a jacket or coat – common in suicides.

- **ISOTOPE:**
  Any of two or more species of atoms of the same chemical element.

- **WARP ONE:**
  A speed of 186,000 miles per second (the speed of light). Einstein said that nothing could go faster than the speed of light – (Adrian proved otherwise).

- **CAPTAGON:**
  A banned substance in America – used by terrorists to remain fearless in battle, no conscience, and to remain awake fighting for several hours, even days. It is classified as an amphetamine.

Neither space or time can be considered independently of one another. They are each components of a single identity, space-time.

The special theory of relativity proposed by Einstein in 1905 was to deal with the preferred status of the speed of light. This theory is the mathematical framework that allows us to extend the familiar laws of physics from low speeds to very high speeds. The speed of light "c" is the maximum possible speed in the universe and all observers measure the same value for "c", regardless of their motion.

Einstein broadened this statement into the principle of relativity. The basic laws of physics are the same to all un-accelerated observers.

Only relative velocities between observers matter (hence the term Relativity).

There is no absolute frame of reference in the universe; no preferred observer relative to whom all other velocities can be measured. There is no way to tell who is moving and who is not.

Time dilation is a prediction of the theory of relativity, closely related to the gravitational redshift. To an outside observer, a clock lowered into a strong gravitational field will appear to run slow.

~David's Journal~

2015:

It wasn't over, the 1993 raid to remove a sadistic and violent warlord whose acts took a terrible toll on the lives of the citizens of Mogadishu, Somalia; the American military who fought to free them twenty-two years ago paid the price, some the ultimate price.

Battles, deafening artillery fire, again screams of the innocent begging for food, sent for their survival by sympathetic nations, only to be massacred by a new warlord and those who followed in a path of violence; they continued to rob the citizens of the necessities for living. The rivers were red with the blood of those executed.

For six years now I still hear their cries ... even in sleep. Did we make a difference returning there? I can see their faces even now. Could I have stopped him?

2015:

Lieutenant Colonel David Eisen and his team prepared to travel to the North Vietnam jungle on a mission to find a missing helicopter and its passengers, an American diplomat, his aides, and the five-man crew, the pilots, gunners and flight engineer among them headed for South Vietnam. Vietnam had been a Communist-Socialist regime since 1975, merging both North and South into one nation. The US had opened a Consulate-General after twenty years when President Clinton was in office, in the Socialist Republic of Vietnam in 1995 in the City of Ho Chi Minh in the South. In January 2007 Congress approved permanent trade regulations for Vietnam.

The diplomat was carrying a briefcase containing a pact between America and Vietnam, headed for the Consulate for a meeting with the Prime Minister Nguyên Tân Dũng and his advisors. The Vietnamese signed a pact in 2013 to allow for a transfer of nuclear fuel and technology from the US to complete its first new power plant by 2014; Russia also contributed. They were now interested in welcoming American oil companies to apply for concessions to search for oil offshore. This would aid the Vietnamese government in accounting for the American MIA's missing since the war. There was another part of the pact that only the South would know about.

On June, 2013, Vietnamese Prime Minister Nguyên Tân Dũng said in a speech that he would welcome the US playing a larger role in tempering regional tensions as China, and some of its South Eastern Asian neighbors would remain deadlocked over competing territorial claims in the South China Sea.

Colonel Eisen and his men arrived a week later with two UN inspectors after the helicopter and passengers went missing; the inspectors would be witnesses as to what happened; the Vietnamese government had granted the search but wouldn't assist. They would try to avoid any encounters of militia that lived in the jungles, above the law, no longer associated with regular army; some had fought in the Vietnam wars; well armed, unpredictable, violent, who recruited others to participate in murders and kidnappings which were prevalent.

The Team would pursue three goals; to find any survivors, retrieve the contents of the briefcase and initiate a rescue if anyone survived. Days later they found the helicopter, a UH-60 Blackhawk; it had crashed into several large trees. Carefully, one climbed the largest of the trees holding it and found the passengers and crew, all had been shot, ambushed by one of the aides to the diplomat then killing himself, gun still in hand; all identification was gathered.

Sunrise joined the Team two years earlier and had climbed the thirty feet having been an avid climber in Ethiopia and quickly determined, with his intimate knowledge of helicopters, having flown several on missions, that nothing mechanical had contributed to the crash. Preacher John Church, a sniper, said a prayer. David then tried to reach two of his men, two new recruits at the jungle's edge without success.

"Something is jamming our radio transmission."

The two men had come under fire while transmitting a message "TIC" on SINCGARS, a single channel ground and airborne radio system to home base; I repeat, "Taking hostile fire"; the transmission was cut short; those attempting to send the signal were dead; the Team never heard gunfire or got a transmission.

Colonel Eisen and the Team, seasoned Special Ops, and having skills in unconventional warfare, were Army Airborne Rangers, some from different military backgrounds and countries, continued on. Two hours later they arrived at a camp. There was recent activity there. They began a search through several structures including a larger warehouse where an arsenal of weapons was discovered; several AK-47s, which alerted them that there might be a terrorist faction there. Other weapons were of Russian and Chinese origin. Then the briefcase was discovered. Half of the contents were missing, then voices were heard; two Vietnamese prisoners were in a 20-foot small structure surrounded by barbed wire and iron and wooden bars; they cried out for help. David and two of his men understood the language. They tried to free the prisoners but were soon surrounded by several dressed in military uniforms, all were armed.

"You are now our prisoners," one said in English, Lieutenant Mao. He escorted the men to the center of the camp. Colonel Minh, the Commander, stepped outside his barrack to meet and evaluate the prisoners.

He looked at David, "Are you their commander, Lieutenant Colonel Eisen," he asked in English, "Orion's Belt?"

"Yes," he replied, wondering how he knew their unofficial name and knew he commanded them.

"You men are our prisoners for the time being."

"We aren't waging war," David told him. "We're with the U.S. Military Office of Investigative Services," a lie to make them not feel threatened.

"I never heard of it … your weapons say otherwise." Colonel Minh knew exactly who they were.

"We're escorting two UN inspectors to find survivors of a helicopter crash."

"Nevertheless, you are in my camp with weapons … you are free to converse in Vietnamese, as you already know the language. Have the prisoners evaluated," he told a medic; "have them fed, placed in the barrack, bring the Colonel to me for questioning."

David tried to remain calm as his concerns were for his men. "Converse in Spanish around the two prisoners in case they're spies for Colonel Minh," he told them quietly.

Two hours later, "Why are you and your men and the UN inspectors in my jungle? It will pay to be forthcoming."

David pretended to give the Colonel all the information, leaving out several details. As captives, they would now wear loose fitting outfits resembling pajamas, serving as prison uniforms.

"We were escorting the UN inspectors to find a missing helicopter, its passengers, if any survived, and to recover a briefcase carried by a diplomat ... we weren't aware of the contents, all classified, then report back to our men stationed at the edge of the jungle ... they in turn would alert home base of what we found."

"Your diplomat was headed South to the Consulate, yet you tell me the information was classified from you and your men ... those who waited for your return at the jungle's edge are dead and no transmission was sent for rescue; you will share the same fate if you do not disclose the information."

David's demeanor changed to one of frustration; he hoped his men, new recruits, were alive and had communicated the attack. "I've told you all I know – you have the briefcase and its contents ... what did it reveal?"

"War," he replied. "America is willing to risk a war to make the South free again."

"We don't want a war with the North." David saw Colonel Minh as paranoid and delusional.

"There are those that do in your government, working against peace with the North. Think on this." The Colonel studied David and his reactions as they talked. "We will discuss this at a later time."

The prisoners now knew about the deaths of the two and no help was coming. They received torture as well as the UN inspectors and were forced to do hard manual labor working from dawn till dusk. They hadn't totally lost hope of a rescue nor a sense of humor. Major Oaloff would often lighten the mood; he was a seasoned mission specialist and next in rank to David.

"We're going to turn this place into a palace and not want to leave when we're finished;" just then he cut himself on the stake holding up a section of barbed wire; he wrapped his hand carefully. "Just a scratch," he told the others, trying not to need doctoring, fearful that one or all of them would pay the price.

"I won't order you to have it looked at," David said, "but you should."

Everyone sustained injuries repairing structures throughout the camp. Rations were sparse and it showed in muscle strength and fatigue. They reminisced about home and family even as their commander could do nothing to improve the situation but voiced his concerns; the men were demoralized.

"They can't produce bowel movements due to no meat in their diets; this steady diet of jungle grain is causing this along with loss of muscle mass," David told the Colonel.

"Come with me." He took him to what amounted to a pharmacy in an area of the medical facility and opened a large cabinet. "This will cure all things related to the stomach and bowels. I believe you Americans call it castor oil."

Several thoughts ran through David's mind. "You've got to be joking." He was about to gag from memories of having taken this as a child.

"All of your men will now have normal bowel movements and in so doing, I will allow chicken to be added to their diets and occasionally meat."

The men did as ordered, none could refuse, and within a week stopped losing muscle mass as they were able to eliminate normally and feel more energetic.

Two weeks passed, a plan was hatched to escape, facing the reality of being killed before a rescue could take place. All had to agree to it. Vinnie, the group's demolition expert, would create a diversion, a bomb made out of fertilizer used to grow crops and animal excrement with some household products he absconded from the storage barrack. Pettigrew, a grenadier, with a specialty in repairing tactical vehicles, would work on a truck motor to provide an escape during the diversion. Days later, there was a signal, then an explosion; everyone ran for the truck amid gunfire. Chan, a drone specialist and gunner, fell wounded but signaled the others to leave. Sunrise went back for him, David assisted.

Colonel Minh arrived and held a gun to Chan's neck. "This adventure will cost dearly ... let him die," he pointed to Chan.

"No," David shouted, "he could still provide the help you need ... he's good with fixing and repairing latrines and sinks;" a lie that saved his life. The men were all punished, from torture to another hour's work every day. Chan managed the plumbing problems with help even without prior experience working with old outdated pipes; his wounded leg would heal.

David was interrogated frequently. Colonel Minh engaged in other tactics as waking him in the early hours to continue questioning him usually over a game of chess and asking what America's plans were concerning Vietnam. "You're trying to throw me off my game," a sleep deprived David remarked.

"I'm attempting to obtain information from you and then throw you off your game."

"You told me not to let you win."

"So I did, yet you do; you have an enemy who alerted us you were coming."

David hesitated then, "I have enemies like everyone else but not everyone knew we were coming here ... is he American?"

"Yes, a special one ... he told us when you were coming and for a price, terminate you and your men, that you and your men mean us harm."

"We mean no harm; you're listening to the wrong voice; are you going to terminate us?"

"I'm not sure ... if I don't" ... he didn't finish. "Remember, if you or anyone needs medical attention or anything during the night, you must present your request to one of the guards – torture will be the penalty for asking ... you will be the one penalized."

He knew the Colonel was serious about not being disturbed. "Any chance for a shave?" Well, while I'm here, I thought I'd ask ... shaving with old razors is hazardous at best."

He was taken back to the barrack, razors were given to the men. David discussed what the Colonel told him about being paid to torture and kill them all by an American, unnamed for now.

"Ivan, it really is you, under all that beard, we didn't know for sure," Sunrise quipped, "but I'll be prettier than any of you if someone will hand me scissors first."

"No scissors allowed."

Ivan was the youngest and a member of the Army CPT, a computer genius and rifleman.

The privilege of bathing had been given the second week of incarceration in a nearby stream ... the prisoners washed their own clothes.

Weeks passed, a search and rescue team continued the search; the men grew weary of a grueling work schedule and consuming grain for most meals and the occasional chicken. Accidents were now common. Preacher John, short tempered and well respected, recruited by David five years earlier, would give a blessing daily having been a preacher, was leaning toward sarcasm at times as he prayed. "Would be nice if you noticed our predicament and got us the 'H' out of here ... Amen."

"Thank you," Oaloff said, "for these words of encouragement Preacher John." He returned the sarcasm to a member of the Team expecting more in the way of encouragement especially when praying for a way out and being an inspiration and encouragement to those that needed it the most.

Vinnie was now nursing an infected foot. When David found out and how long, he had a guard contact Colonel Mihn; it was late evening. The prisoner was now delirious with fever; the medic gave him an injection and David was brought to the Colonel. "I am awake now, what should I do?"

It had begun to rain; David was tied to a tree outside the Colonel's barrack for the night; it was cold, he couldn't protect his men. Thoughts of the two that were killed haunted him. He wasn't punished further. He reflected on the past on how the missions started years earlier.

The General, who now gave him his orders, was commanding an army base in Los Alamitos, a small city in Orange County, California, now known as the Joint Forces Training Base where Special Ops were trained as well as regular army. He took David to live with him and his family after his mother and father were killed suddenly in a car wreck. His sister went to live with their aunt and uncle. He began his college education at USC in Los Angeles in astrophysics, a subject he studied even as a child; he also wanted to join the Army as an Airborne Ranger like his father and the General who had served together years earlier in Special Forces. David was fourteen.

"Take your courses," the General told him, keep up your grades, ROTC as well, get your degree and we'll discuss it; discipline and dedication are two of the rules, the important ones for becoming a Ranger."

Professor Baldwin became David's professor in astrophysics and later had him as TA.

After David graduated, the General discussed options open to him. "I dreaded this day," he said, "you're like a son to Nancy and me ... family. As proud as we are of you, there is always a danger that comes with being in the armed forces. I don't want to see you as a casualty buried before your time, like your father, in a flag draped coffin ... but you have made up your mind, and we couldn't be more proud of your decision to serve your country ... what about Professor Baldwin?"

"Training comes first Sir, then if it works out I will assist him as TA; he is in agreement for this."

"Then let's get you signed up, then we'll celebrate, as a family; those around you will be expecting favoritism from me – there will be none."

"Didn't expect it Sir."

He seemed adamant to taking the most dangerous missions under Commander Costanza Gooding; the General didn't want this for him, but he seemed to need this like an adrenaline rush as each mission was taken.

It continued to rain, he fell asleep.

The next days were tough, his men were losing hope. David saw Vinnie holding a sharp piece of metal that had remained hidden; they were making repairs.

"What are you doing Vinnie?"

"I can't take this anymore," tears flowed as he was about to cut an artery in his neck. "One of the guards took my picture of her and burned it."

"I can't lose you, you're like a brother to me ... I do understand; don't let them do this to you."

"I'll never see them again, facing torture over and over ... I can't."

"We might be rescued, don't give up; do whatever it takes to bring yourself back to her."

"She's pregnant."

"Then you have more to lose if you ..."

"I won't do it ... she needs me, if we get out of this God forsaken place."

"You believe in prayer ... pray."

"I'm not a particularly religious man but I believe in something greater, greater than ourselves ... do you believe in something greater?"

"I've considered that there was something more, but I never pursued it. I'm not a religious man, yet what I've experienced over the years convinces me that there are no accidents ... people suffering, people are killed; there is a reason for remaining alive while others are mortally wounded. I might someday consider becoming religious especially if we live over this." David took the sharp piece of metal from Vinnie. "Preacher John, what can you pray?" David asked him. He had heard most of the conversation between David and Vinnie as he was reworking a stone wall.

"Schwartz," Preacher John said, "pray for us in Hebrew, we need a blessing," he did. He, as a sniper, had enormous respect for Preacher John and his skills. Afterward it was Preacher's turn.

"Let's recite the Lord's Prayer." They did.

Their captors took notice and taunted them, but Vinnie seemed, for the moment, pacified.

The men had been purposely given certain drugs hoping to addict them to obtain more information, but Colonel Mihn quickly rescinded the order when it came to heroin. "They won't live long enough to become addicted." They used sleep deprivation and withholding coffee and beer, at times, instead.

At that time, as David and his men remained prisoners, something entered Earth's atmosphere in the darkness during a severe electrical storm; flaming, it crashed into the Pacific off the California coast. It was brushed off as a meteor, not realizing it was a space vehicle which created the storm. It buried itself deep into the ocean floor. There were scientists who would study it if possible depending on how deep it was buried. Afterward, while it was still dark, one emerged from the ship using a water tunnel to the shore and then disappeared.

At the university, Professor Baldwin and those who knew David, were concerned; no one knew his whereabouts and if he and his men were safe. The Professor was his good friend. Dean Atwell, of the school, brought General Stevens, David's commander to talk with both of them.

"This was a military exercise," the General continued, "Colonel Eisen regularly participates in these exercises but something has gone terribly wrong. Enemy forces have, we believe, captured him as well as others" … not mentioning anything about leading a team. The General fabricated this story of what David's missions were, military exercises, not going into enemy territory doing covert missions. David had also kept this from everyone, including the Professor.

"When will you know?"

"When we find them." The General left feeling very frustrated.

The next day he called a meeting with missions coordinator, Colonel Blake Barnard.

"That arrogant fool got himself and his men captured."

"The Colonel is no arrogant fool, as you called him; he has shown great strategy on the battlefield and on his missions … a genius in my book. No one wants these missions and with a ninety percent success rate you should respect that even if you don't respect him."

Colonel Blake, as he was called, left the room angry. David and the Team didn't respect him and it was evident; he didn't trust him even as they planned the missions. The General never understood the bad blood between them.

He sent others, Army Rangers, as the search was widened; he wasn't aware that Colonel Blake had received a transmission, "TIC," indicating troops in contact with the enemy; he terminated the transmission quickly and never told the General where they were.

Three more weeks passed. As always the men were randomly interrogated; all had various maladies due to being injured or tortured as well as cases of jungle rot due to high humidity. Some still became addicted to pain killers due to more accidents; weed and tobacco were given as rewards for hard work. David was in constant pain from an old injury before their capture and periodically used cannabis or marijuana.

Colonel Minh had allowed his Lieutenant Mao to torture, keeping him occupied. He was young, power hungry and anxious to prove himself.

"But don't touch Colonel David, he is mine alone," he said emphatically. One evening he was brought to the Colonel's interrogation room. "Watch him, I will return momentarily," he told the Lieutenant.

David knew he was in trouble; tied to a chair with two guards, he was at the Lieutenant's mercy.

"You haven't been totally forthcoming Colonel Eisen; perhaps I can prompt you to tell me what you do know." He unbuttoned David's shirt and proceeded to cut him, David cried out in pain, the men heard this but could do nothing. This continued for several minutes; he then moved lower. "Now for the answers or you lose everything." David wasn't talking. Lieutenant Mao made the first cut, David cried out again, tears were streaming down his face. Suddenly Colonel Minh entered the room, his anger boiled, he knocked his lieutenant to the floor repeatedly kicking him; he saw David's injuries, the medic was called.

"Fortunately you will recover," he told him as Colonel Minh listened.

Stitches and a shot of antibiotic were given; he was returned to the barrack the next day, his men questioned him.

"I'm ok, everything's still there."

"Praise God," Preacher said; there were sighs of relief even from the two Vietnamese prisoners as they didn't understand but a few English phrases.

Earlier, each member of the Team left letters for Colonel Minh to be given to their families.

Lieutenant Mao lost a finger for his abuse of the Colonel's prisoner.

Colonel Minh called David in for a game of chess two days later. "This wasn't supposed to happen to my prisoner," tantamount to an apology. "There are those coming for you and your men."

"When? Will we be alive to be rescued?"

"Perhaps ... in any case we must leave here ... you haven't been totally forthcoming with me."

The barracks were rigged to explode so no witnesses could testify. Three posts were set upright for executions. Papers were burned, trucks were loaded to move quickly.

"Why kill the prisoners?" David tried to reason with the Colonel.

Then, "They are coming," Colonel Minh said, "bring the three." David and the UN inspectors were tied to the posts; the Colonel, using his pistol, kills both inspectors then to David; he looked into his eyes as he opens his shirt, "You don't show fear even in this moment ... I will see you again and tell you about your enemy who ordered me to kill you; I decide who lives and who dies ... I decide you live." With that he shoots David narrowly missing his heart. "Let's go," he ordered.

"Sir, the barrack?" one asked him.

"No explosion, no fire."

They left two hours before a rescue came.

Two JH-60 Blackhawks, part of a medical evac, would now take the wounded to a medical facility in Vietnam to stabilize the men's conditions then on to Kadena Airbase in Okinawa, Japan to further have their injuries addressed and begin physical therapy before being transported to Los Alamitos, Joint Reserve Base in California. All had signs of abuse and torture; the bullet around David's heart was removed successfully.

Professor Baldwin received a call from General Stevens. "David and those with him," not mentioning the word Team, "have been found, and won't be on American soil for several days."

"That's the news I've been waiting for," a relieved professor said.

The families of the Team were notified.

Later, the next evening, on the heels of this news, the Professor received a call from a hospital in a neighboring town; he was told that his sister had been in a two car accident and was critical. He quickly packed a suitcase, left a message for the Dean and headed for the hospital; it was late evening. He was tired and stressed. Suddenly he sees a man standing in the road and can't stop the car in time. Quickly he exits the car but can't find who he hit; someone is now standing behind him, he turns, startled.

"How is that you're alive?" Suddenly his cell phone rings, it was his sister.

"Someone has given you the wrong information, a sick joke I guess … I'm fine, got your message an hour ago … are you still coming?"

The professor looks at the stranger, "No, I'm going back home but I'll see you soon, take care, glad you're ok." He didn't mention the stranger. "What is this all about?" he asked him.

"I am not from around here," he said.

"Then where are you from and why aren't you injured?"

"A planet called Vega in the Vegan Galaxy. I am what you would call an extraterrestrial."

"I knew something like this was possible," an excited Professor said. "What do you want with me?"

"I would like to converse with you if time allowed. I need a way in, I need your memories."

"Do you have to terminate me to get what you need?"

"Yes, I am looking for someone you know; he is vital to my mission."

"Are you a friend, because if we could work together …"

Just then he touches the Professor's face and drains his essence; he puts him back in his car and leaves. David learned of his death as he and his men were in Okinawa before they reached home base. Their mission was classified as having been a failure.

When they arrived at the Base, they were debriefed; several from their hospital beds giving an account; all showed signs of torture. The physical therapy was intense. Those that could, attended the funerals of the two that were killed at the jungle's edge, two new recruits who had been on recent missions with David and the Team known as Orion's Belt, Special Forces. On the recommendation of the General, all were to have psychological profiles done and to begin post mission therapy.

They conversed about the mission and now felt they were made scape goats resenting being subjected to what seemed like interrogation tactics. "Tough," Vinnie said, "but the good news is we're alive … and I didn't lose my foot from that cut."

"I bet I can out snipe anyone," Preacher John said, "when I recover from the two broken fingers for punching a guard and the broken rib for sitting too long refusing to obey a guard."

"You're on," Schwartz replied, the second sniper in the group. "How much longer on the weights?" he shouted to a physical therapist.

Oaloff suddenly interrupts, "Here comes Blake the snake," a name given to Colonel Blake Barnard, demeaning his very presence.

"Careful what you say," David said as he was lifting weights to strengthen his back and chest.

"Gentlemen," Colonel Blake said, "how's it going?"

"Till you showed up, stellar."

"Mr. Chan, your sarcasm is wasted on me; the blame for this failed mission rests squarely on Colonel Eisen; those burns should remind you of that."

David walks over to him, "What do you want?"

Pettigrew stands by him, "You sabotaged us!"

"Prove it. There will be a meeting with the General and others next week to decide what to do with all of you. Colonel Eisen, you …"

The men moved closer to Colonel Blake and would have taken their aggressions out on him but David stopped it. "We have better things to do … get going," he said.

Colonel Blake, ever critical of David, would attempt to gain access to the men's physical and psychological profiles to use against them. The missions were put on hold for the time being. The General called him into his office the next day.

"There is to be an inquiry into the deaths of the two UN inspectors and it will be likely that your Team will be split up or worse. David, they're looking for anything and anyone to blame and punish for the deaths."

"And what about the two in our Unit, murdered; Blake couldn't wait to tell us the good news."

"The good news is that you survived … your men believed in you, still do, willing to follow your orders. Each one I interviewed believes this mission was sabotaged. Colonel Barnard is suspected of being involved somehow … and you?"

"I suspect him Sir, not only being involved on this mission but two others."

"There will be an investigation of his activities; keep this under wraps. He is not to be harmed; he's hoping to trap you in some manner and deems you unfit to lead your Team ... we can deal with his attitude later. This doesn't make sense why he has made it his mission in life to see you fail ... I believe this will blow over."

"I hope you're right and for believing in us."

David returns to the University the next day and is introduced to Professor Baldwin's successor. Dean Atwell introduces them.

"David, this is Professor Adrian Rodgers, this is Colonel Eisen who was TA to Professor Baldwin ... they were friends."

"I regret your loss Colonel."

"It's been tough ... good to meet you Sir."

"And you. I need a TA. You were highly recommended and I will work with you as I know your Army duties come first. When did you develop an interest in astrophysics? You graduated from this University with a bachelor's degree 4.0 average, not an easy subject, and became a colonel in the Army Rangers. The military and astrophysics don't usually go hand in hand."

"In the military I am usually analyzing different scenarios used against an enemy and planning strategies, not actively pursuing the enemy; however, things went badly on this last military exercise;" another half-truth to protect himself and the Team.

"Yes, I read about it; regrettable."

"To answer your question, people in my life exposed me to both astronomy and the military ... I wanted both."

"Let's shake on it, a good collaboration." As they shook hands, David became light headed, dropping his papers.

"I don't know what just happened," he said, embarrassed, as he picked up the papers.

"Perhaps recovering from the war games incident and the devastating loss of Professor Baldwin."

"Well, I'll see you later, and I just go by David."

"Call me Adrian;" there was silence then, "I'm looking for temporary living quarters ... any suggestions?"

David turned and walked back to Adrian when he heard this. "You could stay at my place until you find accommodations, better than a hotel. I have a dog, Rex, you'll like him; a friend brought him back from a mission to Afghanistan."

"Sounds good, I'll get my luggage." Adrian was curious.

David was intuitive; something seemed off, but he dismissed it. Adrian, in a handshake, learned more about him than Professor Baldwin's memories told him.

In the time since he arrived on Earth, he had recruited followers, some of which were given implants in their necks – most were looking for a cause.

David started attending therapy sessions with Dr. Ana Cordiero; the men were also required to have regular sessions seeing any of the therapists assigned to them. He thought she was pretty, business like, but had no understanding of what he and his team had been through, but she did. He didn't say much and was evasive when he did talk.

"So you won't talk about it?" she said after sometime, "we have an hour session."

"I have nothing to say … war is hell, people die." He stood up about to leave … he was filled with anger and frustration.

"You have a session next Tuesday." Ana was frustrated as well.

"I'll be here," he said.

He did that again two more times. The General then talked with him; he believed David and his men did the best they could under terrible circumstances in Vietnam.

Earlier, David with the General, visited the families of the two men that were killed on this last mission expressing their condolences and thanking them for their sacrifice. This was extremely difficult. David had never lost a man under his command. As Commander of the mission he answered the questions being as truthful as he could, not giving away classified information. "How could this have happened?" became the most important matter discussed.

"A surprise attack occurred as my two men stationed at the jungle's edge were killed and subsequent capture and torture of those of us who remained after being taken captive," he told them.

"Was it worth it?" another asked who knew all the men had sustained injuries.

David hesitated for a moment, "They believed in the cause of freedom, even to laying down their lives … they believed it was."

Later, he and the General drove back to Base. "Was the cause of freedom a good enough reason?" David asked him.

The General hesitated for a moment, "You know it was … for all of us."

"According to Colonel Mihn, the saboteur was American; he told the Colonel we were coming. Later, he said we would meet again then shot all three of us; he didn't name the saboteur as I stated before, but knew it was Colonel Blake."

"We need evidence … if you can find Colonel Mihn, give us something to go on as to who did leak the information; in the meantime, there will be other missions provided you and your men cooperate with the therapy sessions and are up to it. When you search for Minh, take backup with you … my recommendation; backup should be authorized soon."

"Yes Sir."

"And keep it to ourselves."

The next day David did begin to cooperate. He and the men met regularly after their sessions at a popular bar to talk and unwind. Colonel Minh and his whereabouts was at the top of the list for discussion as well as the therapy sessions.

"We've had information leaked on two previous missions, Africa and Afghanistan; we all suspect Colonel Blake," Pettigrew said, "he's had a power struggle with you especially." He looked at David.

"And where did that young private disappear to who would have received the transmission, if one was sent … Private Bentley?" Vinnie asked.

"The Colonel is a real piece of work. I'll have to admit I wanted to beat him senseless." Oaloff was angry, "And then as much as I hate him, thoughts creep into my head … what if …"

"If he's innocent? We'll just have to get the proof … the General told me hands off the guy!"

"Forget what I just said," Oaloff replied, "I was angry and didn't want to believe it."

"None of us want this situation, but those are the cards we've been dealt; we'll deal with the truth whatever it is ... we'll get proof eventually. The General believes us and is working to get the best lawyers to represent us."

"What about your new tenant, that professor?"

"Professor Rodgers will be staying at my place temporarily until he finds permanent accommodations; we can meet in the planning room if necessary."

The next evening, "I have some parcels and equipment being delivered here ... will that be a problem?" Adrian asked him. "One of the most useful tools to learning is included in the delivery."

"How much space do you need? There is an adjoining study to the guest bedroom." David was patient with him trying to adapt to his new tenant.

"I apologize David, I seem to be imposing."

"No, that's all right ... a machine for learning, I'm curious."

"Then you will be the first to try it." This was in Adrian's plan.

Just then Rex, David's dog, entered the room; curious, he barked twice then walked over to Adrian and sat.

"Usually he takes time to get to the non-barking stage ... I think you've won him over."

"What is he?"

"German Police Dog, he has a history of saving lives ... he and his handler were on missions together in Afghanistan; my friend died and willed Rex to me." David hadn't told Adrian about any of his missions and that Rex was actually his to command on several deployments.

They spent the next day arranging the parcels and other equipment as well as his luggage.

"Your luggage feels like there's nothing in it."

"I do need to replenish my clothes."

David thought this very odd and using the word replenish in that context.

Both had sized each other up. Adrian looked to be in his sixties, grey hair, white, clean shaven, slender at 6'2". David stood at 6'1", slender, muscular, curly short black hair, white, always somewhat tan, mild dark peach fuzz covering his face, blue eyes.

He did have a few minutes under the machine which was part of a reclining long chair with a visor fitting over the face. Thirty minutes passed then the session was over. Adrian helped him to stand, he was disoriented for a few moments.

"You have now had Astrophysics 101, Chapter One downloaded into your mind, the new textbook."

"How is this possible?"

"I designed it and I'll explain in detail at a later time."

Classes began at the University. Adrian brought his own textbooks which conflicted with policy. A few hours later, classes were over and he left with David to meet with Dean Atwell. He had two others on the Board to attend the meeting.

"It's against policy to have your own textbook if not approved by the Board," one said.

"I am an astrophysicist, I can prove everything in this book; years of study have made me patient."

Another on the Board continued, "Two more planets in our solar system, things that travel faster than the speed of light ... we haven't yet achieved light speed; six more elements will be discovered on Earth, three more constellations; matter, as space vehicles, converted into light ... David, what is your opinion? Did Professor Baldwin even hint at anything we've discussed today?"

"I respected the Professor very much; he had his own ideas on astrophysics and proved, with years of research, that they were possible, waiting to be discovered. Professor Rodgers has studied this for years using a higher math to prove what he believes to be in existence or will exist ... I say, give him some latitude to do this ... and he developed the math." David smiled as he said this.

The Board agreed on a trial basis; the two representatives left.

"Thanks for your vote of confidence David; you'll make an even better astrophysicist after learning this new material."

"Can you keep me one step ahead of the students?"

"Most assuredly."

That evening, they reserved time at the school observatory meeting with two other astronomers. Adrian wrote a formula for finding a planet called Vega in the Vegan Galaxy; in reality this was his home planet. In return, he and David got more time with the University's optical telescope as the astronomers studied the information.

After arriving home, David was again given time in the machine. He is very careful where and when he meets with his men; the planning room was very secure. His house was a beach front property less than 1500 feet from his nearest neighbors on the Pacific Coast. It was 2500 square feet, the planning room was 500 square feet added after he purchased the property and garage large enough to accommodate a black Hummer H1, with several improvements, bullet proof glass, run flat tires along with a Harley motorcycle, a pet project which he rode frequently.

He wasn't able to dismiss those feelings that something was off with Adrian. Sometimes at night, he heard him conversing with someone in an unknown language.

Adrian made regular reports to the Vegan Council through a transmitter hung on his wall that looked like a painting; the transmission was routed to his ship then was transmitted to Vega; this was a once a month occurrence. He was vague about his past. No one would have believed he was an extraterrestrial.

His committee, called the Think Tank, formed to do his bidding, was growing; several now had implants in their necks, both students and other followers of various ages and backgrounds not associated with the University. His followers believed that he was human, gifted with unusual powers who would eventually make the world right again.

The implants didn't always work; those having failed implants were terminated. Adrian was executioner. The implants had given him control over a person's mind and will and were a part of him.

David began to follow him as he became suspicious of his activities. He was also meeting with his therapist, Ana, regularly and began to realize that she did care and understood what men and women in war had gone through. The General told him that she had been married and lost her husband in Iraq a few years earlier in a skirmish, killed instantly from an IED. David upon hearing this, was now less hesitant to reveal his feelings; he couldn't tell her everything. He had feelings for her and knew she never dated her patients.

One afternoon, he was tutoring thirty students at the University preparing them for a test. Ana came and quietly joined the group; this was the first time she heard him lecture.

"Does everyone have a book?" he asked. He walked over to her, she was wearing a small scarf worn like a biker, dressed in casual jeans and shirt wearing glasses, sitting behind other students. He handed her a book, knowing who she was. "Chapter 2 page 40. Take notes, the test is Wednesday."

He tutored for over an hour then dismissed the class, he called to her ... "Miss."

She turned facing him, "I wanted to hear you lecture ... I'm impressed."

"You would be if you took this course from Professor Rodgers."

"I'm impressed with you."

He smiled. "Have you ever flown in a military jet?"

"No."

"Sometime I'll take you in one, a trainer; on occasion I fly errands for the General."

"I would like that ... see you Tuesday." She couldn't give him hope; she had feelings for him but he was in turmoil after what he had seen and experienced.

"My sister and family are having a reunion in northern California, Sacramento," he told Adrian. "Come join us; two days off, no missed classes."

"I'd consider it an honor." Adrian was using contractions frequently as he updated his language skills; he knew several languages as he was quickly learning all forms of communication and now, how humans connected within families and groups; texting became a favorite.

"We're an average family; there will be shouting and plenty of fun and then there's the food."

"When?"

"Pack tonight, leave at dawn ... casual clothes, we'll take the jet."

Adrian had gone on a shopping spree with David days earlier and now had plenty of clothes.

They arrived two hours later the next day. Cecily picked them up.

"How was your flight?" she asked them.

"VFR all the way," David replied; he introduced them. "Adrian, this is my favorite sister Cecily."

They hugged, "Your only sister," she replied. "Finally I meet the Professor."

"Just call me Adrian," he hugged her as he mimicked human behavior.

"The view is incredible here as you'll see ... California is a beautiful state."

"I'm seeing it now," he replied.

The house was located where the forest could be clearly seen. Thirty minutes later they arrived.

"We've missed you David," as several gathered around him asking about his rescue.

He introduced Adrian, then "This most recent mission was to have been a war game, military exercise, but we were attacked and held prisoner for several weeks."

"We read about it," Cecily said.

"Since Professor Baldwin's demise, I've been TA for Adrian and learned more than I could have ever imagined. I'll be tested on his textbook and theories next Monday ... he's preparing me for a professorship; believe me, I was surprised ... it's something I've considered for a while."

"That's great ... who's tutoring you? Who will test you?"

"Guess". They both looked back at Adrian who forced a smile.

He was able to study this family unit and David's place in it.

"Prepare yourself Adrian," he said, "it gets wild, but it's family."

Cecily's husband, Grant, was glad to see him, they shook hands. Adrian followed his example and shook his hand. Grant became light headed after giving him access to his thoughts.

"Adrian has that effect on people," David laughed. "Let's meet my uncle, who was like a father to Cecily and me when our parents died."

"And the General," Cecily added.

"Yes, two strong mentoring people."

The afternoon went on, Adrian tasted several foods.

"It's like the first time he's ever tasted food or been to a gathering of strangers", Grant said.

"Probably outside his classroom and comfort zone," Cecily remarked. "You dating anyone special?" she asked David, just then the kids ran by, his niece and nephew; Cecily was pressuring him to settle down.

"At the moment, no. I have someone in mind, pretty, a therapist, standard procedure after a mission … she doesn't date her patients."

"Better get on with it … you do dangerous missions David, more than you acknowledge."

"Now what leads you to believe that?" he hugged her.

"I'm just saying, you have a life, don't lose it out there."

Grant heard that as he entered the kitchen. "Uncle is sitting on the commode nude except for his shirt, cutting up vegetables and who knows what else for the party and rinsing them in the sink, drying them on his washcloth."

"I'm going," she said, David followed. He and Cecily redressed Uncle and thanked him for the vegetables which they quickly hid and brought him into the living room to sit by Adrian.

The music grew louder as activity hit a fever pitch; everyone was snacking and drinking anything and everything. David and an older nephew made time to catch up as they went a few rounds playing basketball.

"I want to join the Army Rangers," he told David, "at seventeen like you did."

"At seventeen, are you sure? You'll have many decisions to make … give it time, finish school, CPA of the future."

"I'm dating a girl in my class."

"Well that's good news … serious?"

"It could be; I told her about you but didn't mention certain things as you said. I really don't know anything until after its happened and you're back. Someone I don't know has been contacting me about you."

"That someone you don't know could be an enemy phishing for information; this sounds suspicious; it could jeopardize our safety and maybe yours ... have you and she?"

"Not yet, and yes, I would wear protection."

"So both of you will graduate soon. I'm proud of you Mike and I would like to meet her. Keep a log of the emails and texts, contents and any names; be careful."

"We don't see you enough ... your missions take you all over the world."

"I regret that. I hope to change some things so I can be with ..."

Just then, "Hamburgers," Grant shouted, "and it's beginning to rain;" everyone ran inside. Adrian, unfamiliar with rain, was reluctant to step inside at first, moments later he did. David observed this.

An hour later, there was a calm as several passed out from the activities and too much beer. David found Adrian.

"You ok?"

"Fine. I've learned from this experience ... I never had a large family." He asked about various artifacts found in the house discovered in areas surrounding the Dead Sea.

"My grandfather was an archaeologist in Israel and was allowed to bring three artifacts he discovered back to America where they have remained here for thirty years."

Adrian asked him to explain the significance of two menorahs and a cross sitting on a table; this seemed odd but he explained. Adrian was forming opinions about the Earth's history especially how religion affected the human race.

The next morning, they returned home; David suggested that they attend a showing of ancient artifacts at the museum that next week.

"Literally telling our history over thousands of years."

Adrian was very interested. "When?"

"After I pass this test."

"You have studied, you should pass it, then to the museum."

He did. He called the General and Ana with the news then Cecily and Grant. Everyone congratulated him including his men, who were getting anxious for another mission. Ana couldn't celebrate that evening so Adrian did by accompanying him to the museum. They were there over two hours as remarkable leaders and thinkers, over thousands of years were discussed, both good and bad. Religion was also a topic of discussion as having a major influence on society.

"It is unfortunate," Adrian began, "that wars never cease, buried under so called treaties, just to resurface somewhere else by those who refuse to learn from the past; so the aggressors are bent on burning history books, murdering knowledgeable men and women who have helped shape this world."

"As if that wasn't enough, they are destroying our history by demolishing ancient cities buried for thousands of years, unearthed, defacing the artifacts contained within their walls so the past can't be studied; this is becoming more prevalent in the Middle East. The Iraqi Mosul Museum was attacked by a terror group recently, Nibus, because they said the artifacts violated Jihadist's radical interpretation of Islam. This has happened in Syria in the city of Palmyra and in the Aleppo Province in Manbij, needless destruction; many of the artifacts are sold for weapons."

Adrian listened carefully to David's comments about war and devastation as he had experienced war.

David called Mike a week later. "I sent you an encryption device to attach to your phone ... only use it when talking to me. Mayla mustn't become aware of our conversations so talk to her or anyone else without it."

"The computer?"

"Communicate as usual ... lure him or her in ... Facebook?"

"I don't think he likes Facebook."

"You said 'he'."

"I have a feeling it's a he."

"The watch will record by pressing the long button ...say at a gathering."

"I like the watch. Thanks. Is Mayla a threat?"

"I can't answer that, but we'll know soon enough and the one emailing you. Keep me posted. I'll check records ... a friend owes me a favor."

"She isn't a radical, no Hajib."

David knew this would be difficult for him.

Adrian was aware that he occasionally smoked a controlled substance and said something one evening as both were grading papers. David was tired and in pain, it was hard to concentrate; he never smoked around Adrian.

"Do you need this substance for pain?"

David became defensive, "I have injuries; the one to my leg was severe, other wounds I can tolerate."

"No therapy, no operation can correct it?"

"Not that I know of."

"I'm concerned …"

"I don't smoke it on campus, the students aren't aware … this is my house Adrian."

Adrian then dropped the subject.

David continued to observe his odd behavior; he had a propensity for space movies and time-to-time shared his fetish with the occasional date or any of his men. Adrian occasionally watched these movies with him; pizza had become a favorite while doing so. He would ask why time dilation or certain phenomena weren't mentioned, or, as he said often, "The information isn't correct; then there's relativity."

David just listened and reminded him, "It's just a show … with these earlier shows, the information simply wasn't complete, but I'll make it up to you where comets, the theory of relativity and certainly time dilation are mentioned."

"Then I look forward to it."

Days passed. Mayla made plans for Mike to meet her friends. She suggested meeting at a bar; Mike drove her. Three young Pakistani men were anxious to meet him, then a fourth, as Mayla's brother joined the group.

One said, "You have a famous relative; fights for freedom all over the world. I heard this from Mayla."

"Be quiet," she said sternly.

"You heard wrong. My uncle only participates in war games; he doesn't do the fighting and honors certain war heroes at various functions."

They dropped the subject as they continued to test Mike for over an hour; they wanted to gain his trust and any information.

"Why not become a Muslim?" another asked wondering if he could be radicalized.

Mayla continued to pursue him which gave her the opportunity to find his weakness.

He called David days later. "I gained more information than I could have imagined. She's the one in control," he said, as he related the meeting at the bar. Then she was planning to meet in three days out in the country somewhere."

"Mike?"

"I declined, too much homework. I recorded the evening's discussions; the encryption device is working just fine … just got three new emails." The discussion would continue at a later time.

David and his men had been in rehab to address their healing wounds from the last mission and build up muscle strength; the last several weeks were challenging. Their fractured bones reflected evidence of torture; burns and cuts were evident. He had hope for full recoveries for all of them.

Two weeks passed. David called Mike. "It took a while before I could get back to you. I have information on your girlfriend and her family. The son and daughter of a Pakistani doctor and his wife briefly moved to England before coming here five years ago. Mayla Ibrâhîm caused dissension to overthrow authority, participated in riots, etc. You seem to be dating an anarchist."

"Her brother Abdeslam is not in any of my classes … we've met, as you know, but he doesn't want to relate to me as a friend or anyone else for that matter; just the opposite of her. The emails began soon after we met; she only texts, no emails from her; but the emails are increasing … almost daily, now asking about your missions, your rank. Then the phone calls started. Always hanging up before a word is spoken."

"You didn't tell me about the calls."

"Mom and Dad don't know … I haven't …"

"They're involved now."

"I wish you wouldn't …"

"I have to Mike. Respect the reasons. I'll be on an interview with you and your Mom and Dad, an encrypted interview, on a specific satellite transmission probably tomorrow … I'll call you … prepare them."

David called the next evening. The interview began. "FBI Agent Scott, Department of Homeland Security, Agents Wells and Burk, Oaloff and myself. Mike, his parents Cecily and Grant are sitting in on this."

"Don't be nervous Mike, we need your spin on this," an agent said.

The interview went on for an hour. Advice was given.

"The watch and email as well as the phone conversations will help us build our case against a possible terrorist or terrorists; good move Colonel Eisen."

"Mike deserves the credit," David replied.

"Those planes that do flyovers and gather information from the internet, to phones, etc. will be directed over their residence and where the other three live."

"Share this with no one," Agent Wells said. The meeting ended.

Days later at FBI headquarters, Mayla and her brother Abdeslam were interviewed.

"We can't prove what you will do. Those planes that do flyovers, gathering information on terrorist activities have in and of themselves given us enough evidence against you Mayla Ibrâhîm that your purpose here was to openly declare your intent to radicalize person or persons around you to commit terrorism as you waged a radical Jihad against your new country. You will be sent back to Pakistan as you will never be allowed to set foot on American soil again. Your parents and brother will be allowed to stay. This is the verdict; you are to leave within 24 hours."

She cried, Mike held her. David and Mike talked.

"Are you angry with me?"

"No … the verdict was severe but justified. I'll make you proud Uncle."

"You already have."

"Remember the symbol."

This puzzled David that Mike made mention of a childhood symbol between the two engraved into a medallion.

The next day, David was informed that Mike left for Pakistan with Mayla. Cecily called him in tears.

David met with the General. "I have to bring him back ... I might be leaving as a deserter but I have to stop this."

"There are two people here who anticipated your reaction to this. You've met them, FBI Agent Scott and Homeland Security Agent Wells."

"Sit, we'll be brief."

"Mike is working for us," Agent Scott said, "undercover as a radicalized terrorist; he has an implant in his arm should we need to rescue him."

"He's too young."

"So were you," the General said. "He's not radicalized – that weapons training you gave him wasn't wasted. He admires you so much, he wanted to be like you. He used Mayla to infiltrate Nibus while she thought she was radicalizing him."

David was tormented, "I'm going to find him and bring him back."

"Then you'll be responsible for his death. Do you want that?"

David just looked at the three. "I can't tell anyone the truth."

"No, you can't. Just say he wanted to be with Mayla and would follow her anywhere even to giving his life for her. You must convince Cecily and Grant that this is the truth. Your own men mustn't know he's fighting for us."

The General consoled him after the meeting.

Two days later Nibus televised their new American recruit who gave a sign for David. It was a medallion around his neck. A sign David would understand meaning, "I'm all right." David managed a smile.

His normal meetings with the Team were planned carefully ... most of the planning was done on Base under the General's supervision; sometimes another location was selected a few miles off Base in David's house in the planning room.

"I'm wondering if Adrian is a spy or just harmless and brilliant ... I know this sounds ludicrous."

"If you feel strongly about something, as you say, follow your gut instinct," Oaloff said, "check his background."

The men were on alert.

Cookouts were a frequent activity as their wives, children and friends joined in the fun; the private beach allowed swimming and beach volleyball which was played very competitively. Business was also discussed as they grilled steak. Adrian was usually at school when these events took place but enjoyed himself whenever he could attend as he observed.

David began following Adrian after seeing several young people on the shore several feet from his house around midnight, surrounding a fellow student; he was tempted to question them or to observe. Adrian questioned the student as he touched his face; there was a scream, then silence. The group dispersed and Adrian returned to the house. David wasn't sure what happened and pretended to be asleep.

Early the next morning he checked the area; the sand showed no signs of a struggle. He found evidence, however, the student's class ring. Adrian is now standing beside him.

"I heard something last night, a scream; did you hear anything?"

"Not a sound … did you find something?"

David put the ring in his pocket and stood up, "Just a quarter, someone lost a quarter … see you in class." He left for the University. Adrian knew David didn't trust him; he would have to deal with the situation.

Days passed, more incidents occurred; one was along the coast. Students and other followers had been summoned to a new meeting place one evening. Daniels, a friend of David's, good with surveillance and photography, watched with him as Adrian welcomed them and then saw them following him into a long tube walkway, made of water, into the ocean taking them somewhere. Two hours later they returned the same way.

"I got pictures of what I'm not sure … care to speculate?"

"Not yet. I need a DNA sample as well."

"Good luck getting it, but if you do get it, Reese can run the tests."

"I'll get it."

The next day, after class, Adrian told David to comprise detailed background checks on all students in his two classes.

"Why?" David asked him, "and how detailed?"

"Very. It will be used for determining their goals ... testing will begin to determine their areas of study."

"I'm against this – you are essentially determining what they become."

"It wasn't a request David."

"Who will see this information and when do you need it?"

"Only you and myself and I need it as soon as possible."

"It will take a while, sixty students ... I have duties at the Base."

"Then it takes the time it takes ... is something bothering you?"

"No; I need to grade tests this evening." He left to add to his already hectic schedule. Adrian hadn't ordered the background checks for his class yet.

Later, as Adrian left the University, he cut his hand on the school door's jagged handle; someone quickly followed and removed the handle and left with DNA.

Reese discussed his findings with David and Daniels two days later. They met in his lab; he was a specialist dealing in the study of DNA and the human genome.

"Not of this world," he told them.

"What does that mean ... alien?" David and Daniels couldn't believe this.

"I'm saying there is nothing on this planet with this DNA. When and where he's from I can't begin to tell you. I would like to study him but at this point we can't ... we could all be in danger and if there are others."

"Then you and Daniels shouldn't be seen with me."

"What about your team?"

"No one knows."

"That might keep them alive; what about you?"

"He knows a lot about me from shaking hands. I felt dizzy and drained the times he shook my hand; coming in contact with him, even the students are in danger." They left the lab with more questions than answers.

David had a session with Ana the next day, it was going well. The men were responding as he was, physically and mentally. He returned later to see Ana when she was alone.

"David?" surprised to see him.

He puts two tickets on her desk. "Go out with me," he said.

"Is that an order or were you asking?"

"Would you go out with me?"

"David, I like you, but it's my policy to never date a patient."

"It's not a date; these tickets were given to me, two hundred each, mid-section, ground floor at the Ambiance Fine Arts." He had purchased the tickets unknown to her.

She looked at the tickets, "La Boehme," she said, "my favorite."

"It would be a shame to waste them; not a date, just good company."

"What time?" she asked excited.

"I'll pick you up here 6:00 tomorrow."

He worked at school tutoring several of the students and grading that next afternoon.

"Where are you going tonight David?" Adrian asked after seeing his transformation, haircut, shaved and new suit.

David now felt that Adrian was the enemy and was careful in what he said; he still respected him, however, even now, wondering what an extraterrestrial was doing on planet Earth. "I'm taking my therapist Dr. Cordiero to see an opera, 'La Boehme'; should be in before midnight."

"This is good for you … enjoy your evening."

David was surprised by Adrian's interest and comment.

He arrived and was walking down a familiar corridor to Ana's office where many therapy sessions had taken place; everyone, who was female, couldn't keep their eyes off him. When he entered her office, she turned facing him.

"Wow," he said.

"I was about to say the same thing about you," she said as he looked at her in a knee length dark green dress. Her blond hair smelled of lavender. To have loved classical music, he had never been to an opera; he made a good living as a lieutenant colonel and working for the General; there would be more opera. As they sat together he held her hand and wanted to know her better, but would she respond knowing more about him.

She enjoyed the evening, he hugged her as he said, "Goodnight" and left her at the office; she didn't allow herself to get too close, not yet.

The next day David invited Adrian on a parcel pickup for the General.

"We'll be flying the jet trainer, probably two hours round trip."

They departed the Base and headed for a supply depot at an airport in northern California. David began to interrogate Adrian as he flew the jet in unusual attitudes now to shake him up; Adrian became angry.

"You said you're from Utah ... there are no records and no college had you on file as a professor; no residence, no family ... it's as if you never existed, then suddenly you're here."

Adrian, who is sitting behind David begins to produce tentacle like appendages which bind his right arm to the seat and another tightens itself around his neck not allowing him to breathe as a third travels up one nostril. He is in pain and about to pass out.

"Place this vehicle into a normal attitude or pass out and die." He does, nosebleed continues. "I'm not from around here ... the Vegan Galaxy is my home. I travelled here to monitor the threat posed by planet Earth and evaluate, contact my people, then decide your fates – turn all of you into harmless creatures or wipe the Earth of all living matter." Adrian withdrew his hold on David as he continued to fly.

"What threat are we to you and your world? We can't travel light speed and we wouldn't reach the closest galaxy, Andromeda for hundreds of years."

"You Earthlings are war like, conquer or be conquered."

"So turn us into sheep, castrate the whole human race?"

"And now you know."

"Now what," he hesitated then, "did you murder Professor Baldwin?"

"I had no choice, I needed his memories and a way in; that gave me an opportunity to teach at the University and meet you, a man of war, I could study you as well as the students."

"When you killed the Professor, you wasted a good life." David tried to contain his emotions over this; had Adrian planned to study him all along?

Just then the jet reached its destination. After exchanging his oxygen mask for a new one and with the parcel, from a small manufacturer at the airport, they continued their trip home.

"Are my men safe?" David asked.

"Tell no one and they will be, since I can know your thoughts and actions by a handshake ... you'll have to stop your missions with the military."

David thought for a moment, "If I do, there will be an investigation and you don't need the publicity. Allow me to go on the assigned missions for the time being."

Adrian considered this. "For the time being and work into your schedule those detailed background checks on the students. Tuesday night come to the shore along Villa Road; you will join the others for a two-hour meeting – these are members of my Think Tank, loyal to me – several have implants and will obey me without question." He didn't elaborate on the implants but David suspected Adrian in the death of a student behind his house in recent weeks.

These meetings were generally every two or three weeks. Daniels and David had two days to find the area in the Pacific near the California coast where it was reported a meteor crashed into the ocean. David slowed the jet trainer to a crawl and after several fly overs picked up readings and recorded a magnetic signature as the instruments in the jet fluctuated erratically.

"That so called meteor is now right beneath us," Daniels said as he viewed his instruments, "covered by at least a hundred feet of silt and rock; you are correct, it's no meteor ... I believe it's your alien's ship and it's huge."

"Let's get out of here," David said.

Daniels would tell no one as he examined and collated the evidence of an extraterrestrial on Earth.

David began to attend the meetings aboard Adrian's ship; he had no choice.

"This isn't astrophysics, we discuss everything ... a think tank of sorts," Adrian had told him.

He was curious. When he arrived, everyone got quiet. Adrian introduced him as David Eisen, his TA. One of the students noticed a tattoo on his lower arm, that of an Army Ranger, and voiced his concern.

"Colonel Eisen only participates in war games ... is that accurate?" Adrian knew better but it was an attempt to belay fears of having a military man present.

"Yes," he replied.

"Glad you could come; take a seat and we'll begin."

David noticed two students from the University sitting in front of him with matching scars on their necks. An older student was introduced who began suggesting ways to stop war on Earth; decreasing the size of the military, decreasing and destroying weapons and large drones with missile capability, having water supplies and transportation cut off to certain areas that produced the weapons, blowing up certain oil reserves, causing power outages. "The road to peace lies within us – we have the ability to show others the way."

Everyone clapped, David sat in stunned silence.

"Thank you Taylor," Adrian said.

When the meeting was over, several introduced themselves to him. He saw more scars on other members, some older, most were students; he talked with them then left an hour later; Adrian talked with him.

"What is this? Suggesting that all problems will be solved by destroying law and order, taking down and collapsing our governments. Brain washing students and adults into sabotage, anarchy, implants?"

"Anarchy might be the only way to save the human race; you're a man of war David, but you're not seeing the big picture ... human beings are destroying this planet."

"Everytime I've been in war it's been to even the odds ... to stop those who destroy freedom, whatever country we're in."

"Then it seems I'll have to change your mind." Adrian looked at him, no emotion.

David and Ana had flown in the jet to some beautiful and spectacular places in California. She began to see the many sides to his personality; he was falling for her. Another opera together. He seemed preoccupied as of late but brushed it off as being tired.

At his next session, "Another mission from the General," he told her.

"But you haven't been cleared for duty," she said, "by me. When?"

"A week, maybe two … Peru."

She knew the General and when he wanted something done he could override even a doctor's decision or timetable.

"I'm counting on having a diplomatic solution on this one."

"I fear for you and your men."

"Physically we have healed … mentally getting better." They talked into the afternoon as he was her last patient.

Adrian didn't try to stop him from going on this mission.

They arrived in Peru, home to incredible beauty, rainforest and drug lords; wars frequently broke out usually between the rivals. They were searching for General Gonzales, considered extremely dangerous. Three days in the jungle, Gonzales' men found them. David had cautioned his men to surrender when captured, they did; this was the usual procedure for a meeting with him. In Spanish he asked to see the General. The area was very fortified, several new buildings and more underground tunnels had been constructed; the house where he lived had been enlarged. The resident community had constructed more housing as their numbers continued to grow. The thick jungle kept the compound from being observed from the air and fortified, for the most part, from rivals who might launch a ground attack.

David was escorted to meet with him. The General stood up, walked over to him and held a machete to his throat as he held his hands behind his head indicating surrender.

"So you thought you would drop in unannounced."

"Pretty much."

Gonzales laughed, "You're going to shut me down … are you?"

"No, but the powers that be are still trying to … and there is a matter of a bell."

He put his machete on his desk, "The Bell of Saint Michaels. Put your hands down, you look ridiculous." He hugged David, "It's been two years."

"More like eighteen months."

"Still too long ... we're celebrating," he told his servants, "bring our guests wine, food, American beer, coca, marijuana, cigars."

"How are things?"

"Tense, but generally good. Rival factions, always a pain ... one of these days you'll make General, a good one; I have a sense about things."

"I wasn't expecting to hear that ... I hope you're right." David looked back at his men.

"Their weapons were confiscated for now and they're having a good time - I am a good host."

"I'll second that."

David and Gonzales went to his study for privacy. "I heard about your mission to find the diplomat in Vietnam ... of course the HNN news broadcast it as a wargame gone bad, not as a failed mission. You were attacked by a rogue militia in the jungle?"

"Two of my men died, I nearly died, we all nearly died. The two UN inspectors with us were executed, as you know ... someone leaked the information of where we were and I suspect on three missions, perhaps even this one ... I'm hoping that isn't the case. When I find who did, I'll kill him. They want you found and shut down; of course that would be a disaster since you eliminate your rivals which is helping us whether they'll admit it or not. Then placing their coca pipelines under your control."

"Only a small percentage now reaches America as I send it elsewhere and it's pure, not that cheap stuff from their factories poisoning those who want it; and still no heroin, not from me."

"We almost catch you, the big lie, only to have you slip through our fingers, so we continue to pursue you." Suddenly, he sensed someone standing behind him.

"Colonel David Eisen, I should say long time, no see."

David stood up, "Costanza?" they hugged.

"What brings you here? You miss us? Sheliah?"

"Does a guy have to have a reason? I was telling the General that we were sent to close him down again."

"Are you?"

"No way." He looked at Gonzales as he said, "We're protecting an ally in the drug war – someone powerful enough to close down the competitors."

Gonzales toasted their collaboration and passed out more cigars.

"The bell?" David pursued this.

"Yes, the infamous bell … it hung above my boyhood parish, it was special; the parish was burned to the ground, agnostics in a battle of rivalry. The priest survived. I took the bell and placed it here until he could reclaim his health and build another church. There it hangs above my gates, very fortified, twenty-foot tall iron gates I might add."

"But you never returned it."

"No, it stirred so many memories, reminders of how my life changed over the years; it represented innocence and innocence lost. I couldn't face the priest knowing, as I am sure he did, my bloodied past … I doubt that he knows I still live."

"What if we took the bell to him?"

"How? It weighs over a thousand pounds."

"But you got it up there."

"Using a powerful crane and it's welded to the gates on either side."

"This would atone for certain things; I'm certain you and your men keep watch over that parish and have fought to protect it … my General would be placated for a while knowing the bell was returned."

Gonzales began to tear up, "We will talk more on this David." Gonzales stood up, "I have to check on something."

Everyone began to relax, old injuries felt better, bitter memories faded. The men were entertained by the women in the large house; dancing and laughter were heard as more beer and Spanish wine were consumed." David and Costanza had some time to get reacquainted.

"You're missed Costanza," David said.

"Looks like you have the right stuff and your men are loyal."

"You miss it … the action? You could still handle it."

"There's a saying, 'you know you're getting old when no sees you as dangerous anymore'. I'm where I need to be, in this jungle fighting the occasional skirmishes with rival factions. You were my best student although I was training a replacement."

"We would have followed you into Hell."

"You did ... several times," he laughed. "When you and your team made that last run in Aleppo on Castello Road delivering medicine and supplies in convoy to the Syrians and all convoys continued to be attacked and the hospitals bombed, I wasn't sure you would make it out of there ... then Vietnam. Some advice ... find time to be a husband, become a father, settle down ... you've given the army everything."

David wasn't prepared to hear this. "I don't know if I can ... someone has been leaking information about our missions. I hope not this one."

Just then Gonzales returned, he heard the conversation and interrupted. "Whoever is leaking the information about your missions, if they come, see what we will do to them." David and three others followed him and Costanza to a large warehouse. "We have this arsenal and much more." They were impressed.

"Where did all of this come from?"

"Your country, black market of course, Russia, Afghanistan, China mostly."

"Hate to hear that."

"We have to deal with who we have to deal with – sometimes I don't like it."

He showed them some old favorites and the latest in his arsenal.

"The M-4 Carbine, 30 round magazine, fires on semi-automatic or three round burst Machine Gun; M-9 Beretta, 15 round magazine, standard issue U.S. Army 9MM Pistol; Glock 19, Compact 9MM Pistol; M-16 Rifle, longer barrel than the M4-Carbine, therefore heavier than the M4; MK-15 Rifle can fire underwater, 20MM, armor piercing rounds; M-17 Scar-H Is a newly fielded 7.66mm x 51mm Carbine/Rifle also fires underwater; the M-240 – 7.62 mm x 5mm belt-fed machine gun, can be carried or mounted on vehicles; the AAI Underwater Revolver and the MK-1 Underwater Defense Gun;

the M-249 Saw LMG, Squad Automatic Weapon – fires 120 RMP weapons with a high rate of fire. We have some AK-47s on hand. Still popular usually carried by the enemy as are stinger missiles, now replaced by FM-92 Stingers used by U.S. Forces; surface to air missiles as the type 91 Kai Anti-Aircraft used by the U.S. are portable, carried by one individual, shoulder fired. Air Defense Systems also include the RPG-FIM-43 Redeye. The RPG-7 is also a portable, unguided weapon, shoulder-fired launched anti-tank rocket propelled grenade launcher; I also have in my arsenal MK-12 Mod SPR Rifles, semi-automatic, and the 40mm M203 grenade launchers that attach to the M-4 carbines. A prototype British 717 would have to be demonstrated, not explained or defined … like having several arsenals in one weapon; and last but not least, the AR-15 rifle. I have supplies of night vision goggles, helmets, grenades, fragmentation, concussion, smoke, optical sights for the M-16s, M-4s, sniper rifles, thermal imaging devices."

He was proud of his arsenal; David wanted in on this and at what cost. David, Oaloff and Pettigrew listened patiently to General Gonzales as he defined his arsenal, explaining what each weapon could do, demonstrating his knowledge of the tools of warfare, mainly to impress them. They were familiar with each of the weapons mentioned with the exception of the English prototype 717.

"I never had to ask my children what they wanted for Christmas," then he laughed, "they are at camp by the way."

"Sorry we missed them," David said.

"Right now it seems like Christmas," Oaloff quipped.

"Can we buy these, especially that prototype?"

"But why on the others. You and your men are familiar and have access to perhaps all of these with the exception of the 717 not only in America but where your other arsenals are located."

"For a rainy day," David was a persuader; these weapons would be invaluable both old and new technology. "Demonstrate the 717."

"Of course … I'll also give you a discount for your rainy day."

"Let's have a beer," Costanza said, "to seal the deal … now how do you boys plan to move these weapons especially to American soil?"

"I'm not sure they're going to America. And throw in those Glock 19s and MK11 Mod Sniper Rifles as well General; three of the 717s."

Just then Sheliah joined the group; she and David had a history. "Sheliah?" he hugged her.

"It's been a while, kept up with you on HNN; no one knows your true identities, no faces seen of the Team solving the problems of the world wherever they're sent."

"We're fighting an enemy within now, sabotaging our missions as of late; almost got all of us killed on this last one. The public suspected this was a war game gone disaster and did give our names, as we were captured, but not captured because of a mission to Vietnam. The powers that be don't understand that General Gonzales is helping to stem the flow of drug traffic into our country by crushing out the competition. We have to make it believable that he's hiding somewhere and no one can find him, or he's dead; and if this mission has been compromised, then we might find ourselves in another war."

This was a reality none wanted to face, but even so everyone enjoyed the evening.

Sheliah suggested a massage for him; both got a massage. She then removed her last article of clothing ... he wouldn't at first.

"Have you met someone?" she asked.

He hesitated, "Not like you, no one like you." Thoughts of Ana were flooding his mind; he had known Sheliah for several years and his feelings for her were strong; they made love.

General Gonzales hoped David and his men would stay and become part of his army; they talked about it. "Perhaps if ..."

"I've considered it, but they would send other search and extraction teams for us ... the men have families, I have family. I could be your best ally if back in the States."

"You are already my best ally ... let's toast."

A very drunk Costanza joins them, "Here's to ..." he doesn't finish and passes out.

Gonzales begins the task of having the bell removed from over his gates starting at dawn the next day. A crane is in place, the welders are busy; a truck is brought where the bell can be lowered. Everyone is excited. It's emotional for Gonzales as he tried to conceal it; he begins to pray.

"If you hear me God, help us not to break the bell … please God, not the bell."

David and the men participate.

"Still can't free the bell," the two said who were on the crane with blow torches. Hours stretched into evening.

The darkness prevented any more work until sunrise. Dinner and relaxation followed.

Suddenly gunfire is heard in the darkness hours later; everyone prepared themselves, some weren't entirely dressed as they grabbed weapons. Night vision goggles and the infrared cameras revealed an army of twenty or more attacking the compound. Gonzales supplies weapons from his arsenal, a second one in his house and arms those staying there. New machetes also replaced those confiscated from David and his men when they first arrived two days earlier. The skirmish was on. The women were familiar with battles and casualties; they were as valiant as the men and tough as they needed to be. Machetes and knives were preferred; most were familiar with the semi-automatic pistols, also a favorite.

The fighting continued, AK-47s as well as an updated arsenal was coming from the enemy side; what followed was a barrage of semi-automatic fire from Gonzales' arsenal of M-4 carbines and fragmentation grenades used with deadly accuracy in a cook off procedure denying the enemy time to toss back the grenades once thrown.

As fighting intensified, several were wounded on both sides, suddenly it began to storm; rain made the odds of the seeing the enemy difficult even with the thermal imaging goggles. Lightening also intensified. As a bolt of lightning struck the bell, it was freed from its bond and flung into the path of the enemy as it flipped end over end, killing several as it continued to chime and roll; finally it came to a stop, mired in mud. Fifteen of the enemy force were killed or maimed; there were injuries but no loss of life for those defending Gonzales' compound.

"No one would believe this," Gonzales said as he looked up to the sky; soon it would be dawn.

"Miracle?"

"I believe so Colonel David."

An hour passed. Everyone who came to attack the compound with the intent of killing Gonzales, was captured or killed. There was a brutal interrogation for the information on who ordered this attack. David didn't approve of torture and this sent flashbacks of the six weeks he and his Team were incarcerated and tortured at the hands of their enemies, but in rare cases he condoned it; he didn't recommend leniency for those who had been part of the attack.

Gonzales, his lieutenants, David and Oaloff met the next day. "I'm not afraid, never have been, to defend my country, my compound, my pipeline; this man, Le Mur, meaning 'the Wall', is their leader and the only man I've ever feared. He's not ever the one leading the raids and destruction; those followers will do it for him. A terrorist pipeline drug lord who pretends to be a legitimate businessman, wears fine suits, drives fancy cars, usually is driven, resides in three countries. France is his country, his home, he has no soul ... I believe there is a contract out on me."

Costanza had joined in the conversation; "An American tipped him off that you and your Team would be here and when, someone on the inside."

"Are you saying a contract has been put on us as well?"

"That I don't know ... as you Americans say, 'killing two birds with one stone'."

"When we return we'll pursue this; he's obviously clever but he can't be above making mistakes ... Costanza, you put up quite a fight; you're still dangerous."

"Think you can outsmart him and not get yourselves killed?"

"We'll give it our best shot, no pun intended; we leave tomorrow."

"Then let's get you packed and one last toast, to stopping a dangerous drug lord and apprehending a traitor who wants you dead." They then raised their glasses. They had a last meal together that evening.

"See that pretty senorita walking toward us? She's my girlfriend ... David, you and your men be safe. I'm where I want to be ... are you returning the bell?"

That night the bell was returned on a trailer in front of the parish. Gonzales and those in the compound reluctantly bid David and the men farewell. No one would know the whereabouts of Gonzales or if he still lived except the terrorist drug lord Le Mur. Several of the state-of-the-art weaponry reached American shores; some were hidden elsewhere.

At a debriefing conducted by General Stevens, "So you ran into a turf war but the elusive General Gonzales was nowhere to be found."

"Yes Sir, but we did knock out a rival's pipeline that he controlled, burned his coca fields and parts of his compound. They had us pinned down for over an hour."

"Glad all of you survived." The General suspected that David wasn't totally forthcoming. "And you want anything intelligence has on Le Mur, the businessman? Why the sudden interest in a suspected drug lord?"

"He was named by a member of those who attacked us and didn't survive an interrogation, as killing anyone who stood in his way to take control of the established pipelines. If General Gonzales still lives, this rival will most likely take him out, saving us the trouble and his involvement in drug activities stopped."

Colonel Blake was in on the debriefing and was frustrated.

"You look disappointed," David said, "sorry we survived it?"

"I can't listen to any more of this; you can't accomplish the mission or won't."

"That will be enough Colonel," the General said, "you're dismissed." A disgusted Colonel Blake stood up and left the room. "The Parish of Saint Michaels sends their gratitude for the return of the Bell. You did good ... let's turn our attention to the next mission. I want you to meet an important member of our team here, Lieutenant Youssuf Mohammad, strategist and advisor; he'll be in on most of the planning stage of this next one ... then we can discuss Le Mur."

They shook hands, he knew Colonel Blake wasn't gone for good.

Later, David met with Dr. Cordiero. Her receptionist had him seated in the waiting room; he wasn't aware of a microphone which was routed to her office, allowing her to hear all conversations of the patients while they were waiting. David began verbalizing his thoughts about Ana.

"If I had you Dr. Cordiero, Ana, I'd hold you softly in my arms after making love to you … I wouldn't sing to you, I can't sing. I would be loyal. I don't have a woman in every port. Sometimes I think you're my anchor."

In a few moments she opens her office door. "Sonya, I'll lock up … come in David; how did your mission go?"

"Good actually."

"No casualties, injuries?"

"Didn't lose anyone, minor injuries, although we're lucky not to have been crushed by a thousand-pound bell we returned to the Saint Michael Parish."

"I'd like to hear more about it."

"You will."

"Well, let's begin." She then sits on her desk facing him; she is wearing a tight black skirt and white button down silk blouse. Her legs are crossed as she takes notes. "I'm going to test your reactions."

"Reactions to what?"

She then unbuttons her blouse, two buttons. "Tell me what you see."

"This is a test?" he said. He thought how pretty she was, but was getting more of a frontal view as she unbuttoned another.

"What do you think of me now?"

"I'm confused."

"About what?" She uncrossed her legs as she unbuttoned another.

"Mixed signals … I'm attracted to you, but you aren't exactly putting out the welcome mat."

"I want you to make love to me," she put down her note pad.

David stood up, "If you really mean that."

She walked over and kissed him as she unbuttoned the last one. He picked her up and headed for the desk.

"No, too many papers … that room over there … the bed."

He turned, heading for the bed, tripped and fell on top of her; both quickly undressed. Her blue eyes met his; an hour of passion for both. She realized he had been tortured more times than he revealed in his sessions. They talked about their pasts as she laid her head against his chest.

"Now tell me about the bell."

David laughed; he would leave out the part about finding General Gonzales as he related the story. "Whoever sent those thugs to attack us knew we were there."

"Who?"

"That's the question. We have faced sabotage on three missions; this stays under wraps – the General knows and I can't reveal even who I suspect."

"I won't mention this, it's not in your chart."

"Lightening freed this bell when we couldn't, from twenty-foot-tall gates, flinging it into the path of the enemy, rolling end over end, chiming as it went crushing most of the enemy, saving our lives. I've seen some strange things but nothing like this; it was almost …"

"Divine?"

"A miracle. We returned the bell."

Ana began to laugh hysterically. "This image in my mind is serious, but very funny … would you finish what you were telling me in our discussion before Peru?"

"Don't you mean session? If you tell me about yourself … I know almost nothing."

"Deal."

"You know basically my story." David related the way the General took him after his father and mother were killed in a car crash. "My sister went to live with an uncle. I essentially was given another family as the General and his wife mentored me. He and my father served together as Army Airborne Rangers. I would follow in their footsteps after graduating from USC with a Bachelor's degree and began basic training to become a Ranger. At eighteen, I went on my first mission. Seventeen years now, made Lieutenant Colonel on a special advancement protocol."

"But why all the suicide missions? You and your men have given up everything, even normal lives."

"I wouldn't call them suicide missions; every mission has a risk. Someone's got to do it … each of us has discussed what normal is and when it's over, all of us have planned a future; three from other countries will stay here. As you know some of the men have wives and kids. I'll continue my work at the University as TA. I'll have a class of my own as a professor."

"You're bright David ... astrophysics is a difficult subject and you graduated early; so you're serious about settling down."

"I was always looking for that special gal. I've been in love, at least I thought I was, but no one wants to build a life with someone who considers the next mission the priority." He stroked her blonde hair which she normally wore in a French twist or a braid when casual.

"I lost my husband in Afghanistan. In special forces he also had most dangerous mission status like yourself; he was killed by an IED five years ago. This was to have been his last mission. He, like yourself, had flashbacks and recurring dreams of his own demise, but he believed he'd get back to me. I decided then to never get close to anyone in the military with that status ... you're chasing a bullet David; you don't realize it as you're leading your men into difficult situations, saving the world."

"I've never considered any of this for glory whether I lived or died. I have secrets never revealed to anyone and redemption seems impossible, perhaps driving me to an ultimate conclusion."

"Could you ever give up the more dangerous missions, even for me?"

"No one like you has ever been in my life. I could, I would and stay in the military as an observer, even to continue planning the missions."

He was sincere; he loved Ana, he fell hard for her. Thoughts of Sheliah were fading, more of a friend and comrade in battle.

Ana kissed him, they went to her condo.

"Grilled cheese?"

"Sounds good ... now tell me about coming to the states."

"I was born in London to an English mother and Spanish father; my parents and I emigrated here when my father became a psychotherapist for the armed forces, treating battle weary soldiers with what is now called PTSD." She continued.

David was fascinated. He considered her analysis of him and chasing a bullet; even so they would work toward having a future together.

"By the way, those paperweights are interesting, who are they from?" she asked.

"A student at school was selling them for his Boy Scout brother. I bought several… I was a Boy Scout." David didn't realize that these glass paperweights were from Adrian given to the Boy Scout's brother to sell on campus. No one knew that each one contained a part of himself, his consciousness, enabling him to see and hear everything.

"They look like a version of starfish," Ana said, "and I swear the one in my office moved."

David was amused; he had given Ana two as well as to the teaching staff, four in his house, not in the planning room and two to Adrian, not realizing that he was the source.

Adrian struggles to control David's activities without an implant. He and two of his men find Adrian's handiwork. From attending the meetings, he learned what he was up to and had received texts from an unknown source, pointing him to certain areas of alien sabotage.

There were monitoring stations in place set up for creating changes in sea and ocean temperature affecting weather changes, causing drought in some areas they speculated, floods in others, affecting El Nino and La Nina systems. Drone facilities were constructed, small but significant, pinpointing the areas of pollution on an unprecedented scale, man-made; a greenhouse effect was in progress. Stopping it or allowing it to happen was in Adrian's hands. He had designs on getting codes for turning our satellites against us, both communication and weapons capable, as he stated in a meeting; the Vanguard was one.

David convinced Oaloff and Pettigrew that Adrian wasn't a spy or a terrorist but was brilliant, a scientist who had invented things to control the weather and harness energy, installed without government approval and needed to be dismantled; all those facilities wherever an unknown follower of Adrian's gave locations.

David attended every meeting that Adrian's followers attended, disagreeing with those who had implants or were waiting for theirs. He tries to cause dissention and split the group now numbering thirty.

Three students were now planning to murder him. Halfway through this evening's meeting, Adrian has everyone take a break.

"Colonel Eisen, I'd like to discuss something with you."

David followed him into another room where he saw the machine for implanting a person; he hoped to escape that fate. "So, this is where you do it."

Adrian was angry. "You have been a disruption at these meetings and have sabotaged my efforts on behalf of Earth."

"Like turning the Vanguard satellite into your personal communication device to your home world, interfering with our eyes in the sky and turning these into monitoring everything here on the planet, including climate change and changes you're affecting on us; then turning our weapons against us … you're going to destroy us one way or another … maybe someone here, at the meetings, will figure it out, that something is wrong." They continue to argue.

"Let me read your mind."

David refused, "You sorry bastard."

"What is that word?"

"Look it up in the dictionary … you lied to them, you lied to me; you murdered my friend, Professor Baldwin, and others; the implants must have malfunctioned on at least two."

"I don't care for your tone David … and where are those profiles on the students?"

"Fight me, put away your powers and fight me like a man."

"I'll show you to be disruptive … you and your men have destroyed several facilities I constructed … this will stop."

David threw the first punch knocking Adrian against a wall; he wiped blood from his lips, red blood. "Don't put one of these things in me."

Adrian now throws the next punch. They go at this a while longer, arguing more; after several minutes Adrian releases an energy surge knocking David against a wall, he fell to the floor. He hesitates for a moment as he looked at an unconscious David, then calls in two students who were planning to harm him.

"I need your assistance … bring him to the table, the Colonel is getting his implant tonight."

"He's military, why don't you just kill him – let's kill him for you."

"The implant will give us control; he brings much to our organization and information regarding the military and their weaknesses. It isn't necessary to terminate him ... if he is harmed, you will pay with your lives."

"We want to watch at least."

"I want you both to lead the others into forming ideas for our next moves; sabotage, recruitment and so on. Tell your friend Billy what I have told you and to sharpen his cyber skills. I have a job for him. The implant will be complete in a few minutes ... you may leave now the Colonel is ours."

They reluctantly left; the machine was about to deliver the implant attached to a long device, the shaft, into David's neck under the hairline. Adrian, moments before, pulls off the implant, allowing the device to leave a scar matching those of the students; the implants were a part of Adrian by which he could control his followers. Afterward, two assisted David to his car. Adrian drove, they were alone. David had been anesthetized and was now coming out of it; he was aware of what Adrian had done to him.

"Damn you Adrian."

"I warned you; it seemed the only way to keep you in line."

Adrian was distracted and ran a red light. It was late evening, the police pulled him over, lights flashing.

"Use your power of persuasion now Adrian," David said.

"Where are you headed?" the officer asked him, "you ran a red light."

"I was taking an associate of mine home."

"He seems incoherent," the officer said.

"He's just had a procedure and is under the influence of an anesthetic."

"He did this to me, the procedure ... he's an illegal alien."

"Alien? Get out of the car. License and registration Sir; are you an illegal alien?"

Adrian was able to produce all the information. "He's my assistant at the University ... I'm not an illegal alien and certainly did no procedure on my associate."

"Everything seems in order," one policeman said.

"He's an alien from space," David yelled, sounding drugged.

"You better get him home, he's definitely delusional ... I'm letting you go with a warning – watch the red lights."

"Thank you Officers."

Once home, Adrian assisted David upstairs; his frustration was evident. As he came to himself and studied the scar, knowing he was changed, he began to shower; within moments he punched through the glass shower door, venting his anger, severing an artery in his arm. He fell as he passed out from loss of blood. Adrian knew something was wrong as he quickly went upstairs; he stopped the bleeding then turning off the water, he placed a quilt over him then proceeded to read his mind as he laid there semiconscious, learning where and when he received his injuries over the years and now knew the faces of all those he commanded.

The next day David was leaving for the University, not mentioning his arm. "I called the glass company." he told Adrian.

He responded by asking about his injury, "Are you all right?"

"You should have let me bleed out, you've destroyed me." He left Adrian wondering how he would deal with him.

As David was grading papers at school that afternoon, a student came by. He was in one of Adrian's classes and a member of the Think Tank which encompassed all of those, including David, who followed him.

"Colonel Eisen, do you have a moment?"

"Yes, come in Seth; you did well on the test."

"That's good news ... to get to the point, you've disrupted every meeting since you joined us and I feel, because of this, I can trust you."

"I'm listening."

"You are aware of this, that the Professor is making changes to our atmosphere ... weather changes spell disaster for our planet. You're not one of us yet, so ..."

"I have an implant; the rumors are true. I wasn't falling in line, but I can still think independently, for how long, I don't know. I have a climatologist friend who agrees with what you're telling me."

"I am trusting you with my life. I know where more of the installations are responsible for these changes … I am willing to show you where, then do as you decide. I suspect you've already sabotaged what I told you about earlier."

"Does anyone else know?"

"Taylor suspects that I'm against this … he's dangerous; he believes my implant isn't fully functioning."

"I'm familiar with Taylor … the only thing he respects is power and violence. I'll bring a map and we'll find a time for you to tell me in detail where they are and a description of other devices." David had a genuine concern for Seth's safety. "I'll call you." They did meet a week later.

David met several times with the General as more information was gathered on two upcoming missions; he continued attending the meetings required by Adrian; those in the Think Tank began to accept him as he became less disruptive. The detailed reports on the students were discussed, reports which enabled Adrian to find fertile minds willing to commit to him and directing their activities. He would also encourage those overseas to apply and receive scholarships, in some cases, for his Astrophysics classes and become part of the Think Tank.

David knew that Adrian had the identities of his men. He still met with them regularly about a mission he was pushing for, to find Le Mur; the General hadn't approved it yet. David had temporarily held back on sabotaging Adrian's efforts, but kept surveillance on his activities. Oaloff and Pettigrew would assist David as needed to disable his handiwork; he hoped his men would be spared retaliation.

David had brought Ana to some of the socials, usually cookouts, where the men, wives, girlfriends, and children were invited; there were rumors of marriage in the works. As always, business was discussed. Sunrise, who had tattoos of every woman he had ever dated, showed his latest one along with the woman he was engaged to. Everyone congratulated them.

"When for you guys?" One shouted, looking at Ana and David.

They smiled, acknowledging nothing yet; there was a call from the General as to where Le Mur was going.

"He's planning something – come by this evening, bring the Team. There is an update on Warrior's activities in Liberia." They met.

The next day, on his way to the University, David was followed.

"Don't turn around, no weapons ... walk; you follow instructions as well as you give them Colonel Eisen. Now that we have privacy, why are you pursuing me?" Le Mur removed his sunglasses as he talked with him, his two bodyguards were close by. "I have been followed ... the beggar with a tin cup kept tabs on me in New York ... I made a generous donation to him and his dog; another of your men parked my car, adding a tracking device which was found quickly. Argentinian limo drivers are loyal and observant, your driver wasn't familiar with certain aspects of my route; he could have vanished easily, but what a waste. These people, I assume, you hired, not from your Team ... what do you want, I have no quarrel with you?"

David was startled by the terrorist, but remained calm as he answered. "You are a terrorist. General Gonzales has been repeatedly attacked for control of the pipelines he has acquired. Those whose loyalty you can buy will fight to the death. He is helping to stem the flow of drugs into our country, drugs with impurities; we have the intel on your activities as you start wars to place people in power to do your bidding, even here."

"All you've said is true, but what can you do about it? I could have you or your men eliminated. I order assassinations, I order war and I do occasionally respect the opposing team. Plane crashes are part of the plan in some cases ... remember that. I will never be caught ... I hold in my hands cyber warriors who could do great damage to your country's national security."

"What's your next move?"

"You present a challenge to me ... General Gonzales might be spared. As far as the next move, I'm not so sure; stay well you and your men."

Le Mur and his bodyguards left. David knew he had been getting intel on him and his men. This tall, white haired man with a ponytail unnerved him; would he back off, should he?

"Lucky to be alive, all of us," Pettigrew said as they discussed that meeting, "but face to face, even letting you live."

"I think it's a game to him."

David told the General who was very concerned and stepped up security at the Base and for David and the Team; all refused. "I don't sense an eminent attack on us personally, unless he feels threatened."

"Nevertheless, I'm contacting our agencies around the world to give us more intel on him and what he might be up to."

Adrian and David were now boarding a flight to England pursuing a possible recruit; the two had a fragile truce as David continued planning how to stop him or destroy him. The pursuit of Le Mur wasn't permanently postponed, knowing how dangerous he was.

Just before takeoff, four men boarded the jet; an elderly man then complains of heart palpations and was carried off by paramedics. The jet began its takeoff roll, David got a call from Ivan who was stationed at the airport.

"Le Mur was carried off the jet by paramedics, I know it was him; he removed a fake beard and wig then looked in my direction and disappeared." Just then the jet began climbing to altitude.

"There are terrorists aboard, I suspect three, maybe four," David whispered on his cell.

"Should I alert anyone?"

"Not yet."

An hour passed. He continued to watch a forth passenger who seemed to know the others as they were staggered in their seating, not sitting next to each other; two were very nervous, all four of Middle Eastern heritage wearing casual clothing. Minutes later an announcement; two stood up.

"Everyone be quiet, we are commandeering this jet … be still and no one gets hurt; we will be going to a new destination."

"Who are these people?" Adrian was concerned.

"They're terrorists, probably using us and this plane as a bargaining chip. The man who was taken off the jet is, in fact, a terrorist, but he escaped the fate that we face, probably orchestrated it. We will most likely be flown to a terrorist country to be bought or sold, it won't be Britain."

"Explain further."

"Shut up," one of the terrorists shouted, pointing a gun at Adrian.

"What do you want?" a soldier in uniform asked.

The terrorist in charge walked over to him, "Stand up and empty your pockets. Looks like you're headed to our land to fight us."

"I was going to Britain before you changed course on us."

"You wear the uniform, are you willing to die for it?"

The man hesitated as he looked into the face of pure evil, then, "If I have to, I will die for it."

The terrorist shot him. David stood up, but it was too late to help.

"And who are you?" He searched David's pockets. "Army Ranger with a Jewish name... I sentence you to death on both counts."

"Wait," Adrian said, "we can come to an agreement."

Suddenly, one of the pilots was shot; the other had cooperated making the course changes. David was pistol whipped and thrown back in his seat. Adrian urged them not to execute him.

"Jets are being sent as we speak," another terrorist told the passengers, "this won't become a hostage negotiation after all; point the jet toward the ocean." He said a quick prayer to his god as he looked over at a comrade who opened his jacket, revealing TAPT explosives, hidden until now, smuggled aboard with four guns by a workman and put in the galley ceiling.

"Can we win with these people? Are you all right David?"

"We're about to die; you can't reason with a terrorist."

"Why?" Adrian asked them.

The terrorist in charge smiled and turned away. David and two others got out of their seats, attempting to stop them, then the explosion as the jet hit the water. Adrian, in a microsecond, had quickly put a force field around David, himself and those toward the middle of the jet; they helped to save any survivors, helping them climb on top of the pieces of the jet and other debris until help arrived. They climbed onto a part of a wing when no more could be saved.

David wondered if Adrian cared for these people – did he view death as humanity did. It began to rain as a storm approached.

Suddenly, one of the terrorists who had somehow survived, tried to climb onto the wing, he had a gun. David fought him, then both fell into the ocean; the terrorist drew his gun even as David had him in a choke hold suffocating him. Adrian was prepared to assist if needed. The cold ocean and rain were too much as he couldn't grab hold of Adrian's hand, memories of his captivity in Vietnam began to resurface. As he sank beneath the water, Adrian grabbed him, pulling him onto the wing; the storm was unrelenting.

Several hours later, all was quiet. David awakened and saw Adrian sitting, staring at the stars.

"Did any make it?"

"Yes, several ... I have sent a signal for rescue."

Just then David leaned over the side of the wing and threw up; they were going on their second day – he was in pain and now confronted Adrian about the implant.

"You don't have an implant."

"I have a scar."

"I saved your life. Three of my students were planning to murder you unless you had one; only the scar identifies you as one of mine."

"No implant ... but you know I sabotaged six of your facilities."

"I want those who assisted you."

"I'll never tell you."

"I already know."

David threw up again.

"Can I assist you somehow?"

"You asked me why I smoked marijuana occasionally – the truth is what I told you, injuries from previous missions require some relief. Not having it now is a form of withdrawal, another downside and no relief ... you saved my life and several others to live another day. I don't think you can help me at this point." He rested his head on the coat of his new suit continuing to deal with the nausea ... "These outfits are probably gone." Then, "Don't harm my men."

"I'll need something in return."

There was silence then, "Tell me about Vega, you've never described it."

Adrian moved closer to David and sat, "All right." He pointed to a direction in the sky. "You can't see it, even with a telescope ... life is very different."

David's eyes are closed, Adrian fills his mind with visions of his home-world and temporarily stops his pain.

A day later a rescue; several were saved, having given their thanks to both for their help. They returned to the University; everyone knew they were aboard the downed jet and their participation in saving lives. Adrian begins to understand what being a terrorist meant, that all people aren't the same. David suggested that he watch HNN as often as he could to see what current events were happening around the world; the atrocities that were being committed against defenseless citizens, especially by terrorist factions and by ruthless dictators causing mass migrations to escape the death and destruction. He began to form other opinions about war and why they were fought. There were also the presidential debates, which he found humorous.

"It's not all bad," he said, "but no one is in agreement; the world leaders can't seem to stop wars, even as they criticize one another."

Le Mur calls David, "Neither you or your friend were supposed to die on that flight – a miscommunication with the leader of the four; good help is hard to find these days ... I was hoping, however, that all passengers be detained in Pakistan, held for an undetermined time, the usual red tape, but especially one, Colonel Eisen."

"Why did you leave the plane, knowing one of my men could identify you?"

"Essentially to let you know who was in charge. Don't become a problem that I'll have to eradicate ... as for General Gonzales, we will work out our differences one way or another."

David listened very carefully and was about to reply, Le Mur ended the call, it couldn't be traced. He called General Gonzales and related the news ... "The professor and I survived with several others. Le Mur will be paying you a visit ... a negotiation, he said."

"I will handle it Colonel David ... be well." Le Mur was there.

David now had to convince the General to leave the situation alone while still monitoring his whereabouts; and still no mention of General Gonzales who was presumed to have died months earlier.

Adrian was deciding what course of action to take as the sabotage of his weather facilities continued and now a transmission station to jam our satellites knowing David and his men had been involved. He still stuck to his plan of blind obedience; the implants would turn mankind into obedient sheep, or if all else failed, the total obliteration of life on earth.

They again travelled to France, Dubai, and Britain to lure three students to Adrian's Think Tank by giving them full tuitions paid for degrees pursued. David couldn't interfere as they agreed to Adrian's terms and generosity.

While in Britain, Adrian, after procuring the third student and visiting five areas of London, took David to visit Cambridge University. They went inside and were met by an attendant.

"He is expecting you Professors." They walk down a long corridor which led to a conference room.

"Who is it, Adrian?"

"You're about to find out."

As they enter, another attendant introduces them to a man in a wheelchair.

"Professor Hawking?" David wasn't expecting to meet him, but pretended otherwise.

A computerized voice welcomed them, "Glad you could come. I have the upmost respect for pioneers like yourselves and wanted to meet you. I have given my life to being a theoretical physicist. In 2009, I retired as the Lucasian Professor of Mathematics to become Director of Research of the Dennis Stanton Avery and Sally Tsui Wong-Avery Department of Applied Mathematics and Theoretical Physics, working on basic laws that govern the universe."

"A Fellow of the Royal Society and a member of the US National Academy of Science," Adrian said, "speaking of pioneers.".

"I am anxious to hear some of your theories … and pardon, I can't shake your hands."

Adrian walked over to him and touched his hand for a few moments. Stephen became light-headed, his eyes met Adrian's as he realized in that moment that Adrian was different, unique. David then touched his hand, David also seemed different.

"David is my protégé and an astrophysicist in his own right."

"Not nearly in his category or yours Professor."

"You're too modest … don't put a ceiling on yourself or your quest for knowledge."

David looked at Adrian, "I won't."

"I am changing some of my views on black holes; my black hole theory was a blunder. I have worked on the basic laws which govern the universe. Roger Penrose, a colleague, and I showed that Einstein's General Theory of Relativity implied that space and time would have a beginning in the Big Bang and end in black holes. These results indicated that it was necessary to unify General Relativity with Quantum Theory. One consequence was that black holes should not be completely black, but rather should emit radiation and eventually evaporate and disappear. Another conjecture is that the universe has no boundary or edge in imaginary time. This would imply that the way the universe began was completely determined by the laws of science. I believe now that light and information may be able to escape from black holes … what do you think?"

"Is there a single unified theory combining Einstein's theory and quantum mechanics into a single quantum theory of gravity? The unified theory which would resolve all the mysteries left unsolved? I don't have all the answers." Adrian, however, did.

"You have written a textbook using higher math you developed. So many discoveries from more elements to more planets in our solar system and so on. The speed of light exceeded?"

As they communicated, David and the attendant listened intently as each topic was covered and mathematically scribbled then on two chalk boards.

"If I tell you all the answers, there are no surprises waiting. You have dedicated your life to this; they call you the most brilliant theoretical physicist since Einstein with ground breaking research in black holes. I will tell you, the best to be discovered is in your grasp."

"Funny, you would say grasp … I do have a sense of humor. A single observation has all but nailed down a primal explosion, the Big Bang occurring 13.8 billion years ago. This was the observation made by a team of researchers headed by astrophysicist, John Kovac, at the Harvard-Smithsonian Center for Astrophysics. It has confirmed the existence of gravitational waves and the inflationary universe. Those waves were first described by Albert Einstein ninety-nine years ago who envisioned space-time as a sort of cosmic fabric that could be warped and jiggled. The inflationary universe was theorized in the 1980's by physicists. It was theorized that in the beginning, the universe expanded so rapidly it actually exceeded the speed of light. If the right kind of jiggling could be spotted, it would prove both gravitational waves and inflationary universe and support the Big Bang in the process. But they didn't see jiggling. They saw, with the help of the Background Imaging of Cosmic Extragalactic Polarization-2, or BICEP-2 instrument at the South Pole, was a distortion in the microwave radiation that pervades the cosmos, like ripples in a pond. Those ripples were powerful enough that they likely came from an inflationary universe that produced gravitational waves which were set in motion by the Big Bang. Their work still has to be replicated by other researchers," Stephen told them. "It is an exciting time, no matter whose discovery it is … we all want answers."

The chalk boards were soon filled with equations. Stephen and Adrian agreed then countered one another several times.

They broke for a late lunch. Stephen took his in the form of a liquid. More discussions followed.

At the end of the session, Adrian took Stephen's hand. "Open your mind to all of this; travelling the speed of light and beyond is possible; a future of space travel beyond the stars, even black holes … new theories you have been working on … a future beyond comprehension."

"And alien lifeforms," Stephen said looking at Adrian.

"What do you think?"

Stephen smiled, "Until we meet again."

Later, "Did you tell him?" David asked.

"He knows about me, not about Earth's future."

They left for the airport to return home and welcome the students to the Think Tank. Shortly after they arrived, all were given implants.

David and Adrian argued over this, "You've ruined their lives Adrian."

"In your opinion," a frustrated Adrian replied, "and where are you going, to fight another war?"

David was quickly packing. "A rescue mission … Liberia. I'll be gone four days … Ben will substitute as TA while I'm gone."

"I forbid you to go … I know who your men are, I read your mind, or have you forgotten?"

"I am going and they're going with me to save hostages before they're executed. If you're going to stop me then do what you have to do, otherwise I'm going; there are those counting on us."

The conversation abruptly stopped as David finished packing his duffel bags for the long trip and left for Ana's where they would spend one last night together. Adrian didn't try to stop him even as he knew the dangers of his missions.

The mission plans were finalized the next morning. Lieutenant Youssuf Mohammad was in on the planning of this one; he had been in on other missions before working with David and his team under General Stevens. He had taken the role of mission planner over Colonel Blake for the reason that he was connected to the area. A nurse captured by the most wanted of three terrorists in charge had given intel to the American rescue team at the risk of her life. She had been working with a doctor to tend to those civilians and soldiers from both sides who were wounded in a land grab by this terrorist faction, Nibus, as a takeover took place in this Liberian town which was held hostage.

Al Qaeda was in Liberia and other parts of Africa as well as Boko Haram who had allied itself with Al Qaeda against Nibus who began a conquest there. International terrorist organizations were active on the African continent. Al Qaeda in the Islamic Maghreb and Al-Shabaab in Somalia. The terrorists in Africa wanted to recruit followers, many unwilling at first, to seize control of important resources like oil and diamonds as well as uranium; drug trafficking continued as an important resource. Since 2,000, Sierra Leone, an area of Liberia, became an important source of diamonds, blood diamonds. The former Liberian leader, Charles Taylor, was found guilty in the International Criminal Court in The Hague for fueling the war in Sierra Leone.

The terrorist attacks in Kenya, Nigeria and Liberia have now focused the attention of the international community on the renewed strength of the terrorist groups.

A school was destroyed to discourage learning; several students died and several were wounded to discourage opposition. The area was also plagued by a new disease as well. The two story brick hospital had survived major attacks; all five rooms were filled; an attic was the supply room. The doctor there was assisted by Genet, the nurse in charge and five others who had nursing experience. She and the doctor would pay their liberators, once freed, with a cure for this new disease; no one else was aware that a cure had been developed.

The team was now approaching, several miles away, in a UH 60 Blackhawk with a Humvee towed in sling load beneath. The intel they received from Genet, on the inside, would determine how they would proceed liberating the captives and capturing or terminating the three terrorists in charge; they needed the leader alive if possible, only known as Warrior, who embraced radical Islam as did his followers. Lieutenant Mohammad knew the terrorist leader as an ex-follower and would identify him. The town and its citizens had been held hostage for nearly two months The Lieutenant was Genet's husband; they had a child, also a captive. She pled with Warrior that their three-month old child be spared; he had repeatedly raped her so she would deliver another child, his. He had considered using her as a bargaining chip to release other imprisoned terrorists though he was in love with her, a distorted love.

A drone, equipped with heat sensing, infrared cameras, operated by specialist Chan, would give an overall view of the terrorist positions and the captives as well as document the destruction of parts of the town and the carnage that followed of both young and old.

Preacher John, Vinnie, Schwartz and Chan were now stationed on a hill a half mile away. The Humvee was able to negotiate the twenty miles where the drop off occurred through rough terrain to the hill and was parked some distance away until needed. David and the others walked the distance from the hill to do a recon of the terrorist stronghold using intel from the stealth drone, a prototype that made no sound. Any radio communications, between the men, were in code and Spanish.

"We need communication from her," Oaloff said.

David shared his frustration. "For all we know he might have killed her."

They sent a small beeping sound to her transmitter. Moments later she sent an S.O.S. to them with a code number that only she would know.

Preacher John prepared his sniper rifle for a kill shot or whatever was necessary.

"We've done a quick recon as best as we can, the place is crawling with Nibus and insurgents who joined them ... willingly, we don't know. Bodies of students and teachers have been left to rot on the school steps as a reminder of what they can do. Several civilians are working and their children to do anything they're told. Genet has given us up to date intel and will identify which one of the three masked terrorists is Warrior. I need to talk with Preacher," David said.

"Copy that ... Preacher John seems to have left us, his rifle jammed."

"Shit ... find him."

"The truck," Chan replied, "he has to be there."

"Find him."

Two went, Chan and Vinnie. Preacher was on his way back when attacked by two villagers, allies of the terrorists; help arrived but not before he sustained injury from a chemical sprayed in his eyes. Chan finished off the two using two machetes at lightning speed before a shot was fired. They returned to the hill with Preacher and his number two rifle.

"He can't fire the rifle, they sprayed something in his eyes ... he can't see, we're flushing his eyes with water."

"Temporary?"

"Don't know, Sir."

"Preacher, you wandered away ... you okay?"

"That depends ... careless of me ... I can't see. My number one jammed, went back for number two, then attacked."

"Keep hydrating your eyes 'till we get help ... put Schwartz on."

"Colonel."

"You're up, Buddy," David said, "lock 'n load."

"Copy that." Everyone prepared. Doubts filled his mind, Preacher encouraged him.

"Listen, you have this, a designated marksman proficient in using a range of weapons and sniper rifles, you might beat my distance record; we'll go step by step." Preacher's rifle known as his number two was one Schwartz was familiar with. He would use it considering that it was good luck. They did, zeroing the weapon, adjusting for range, wind, target detection, moving target estimation.

"What if I hit a civilian?"

"You do what you have to do to free those people before anymore are slaughtered ... I understand your reasoning, I went through this, but several were saved." Schwartz was prepared.

David had joined Mohammad and Sunrise initiating a ground attack first, "Weapons hot ... fire," he shouted. Oaloff and Pettigrew were also initiating ground fire outside a tent as they protected Ivan inside, not sending a satellite transmission as he siphoned off data from three computers used by the terrorists.

"Ivan?" David reached him by radio, "get out now, troop movements headed this way."

"Not just yet, Sir. I'm still collecting data; money transfers to the terrorists naming those countries and those around the world who have paid them to do their bidding for profit... you wouldn't believe."

"Now," David said.

"One more thing." Ivan sends a coded virus to the computers of the enemy to delete everything and destroy the hard drives. "Now we're finished." Just then a terrorist enters about to fire on Ivan and Oaloff.

Pettigrew stabs him.

David heard everything. "Move east, wait for us."

Sunrise had moved farther into the camp and found two trucks with a capacity of carrying twenty-five.

"A no go on these trucks, they're rigged to explode, basically setting a trap for us."

Had Genet been discovered disclosing information from a hidden transmitter, she would have been executed. She contacted the team again giving strategic information of where the terrorist guards were and where other children were taken; several had been sold to increase revenue.

It was time, Mohammad and Sunrise revealed themselves as part of the plan. David was communicating with Mohammad through an earpiece. The three terrorist leaders were caught off guard by their willingness to subject themselves to certain death.

David's last communication was, "Identify him, then find Genet and the child, bring them and the doctor to the second building."

"On your knees," another terrorist told them as he took the earpiece.

Mohammad couldn't point out which one to Schwartz, his hands were bound behind him but he knew which one; he would have been shot before he could signal. All three terrorists, faces covered and armed, approached both.

"So you returned to me."

"So I did," Mohammad replied.

"You came for her and the child; the child will die as will you."

The mission was now a life or death struggle. Those that wanted Warrior for interrogation were willing to do anything to get him, dead or alive – preferably alive.

As Genet is about to transmit which one was Warrior, someone is now standing behind her with a knife, one of the nurse's aides.

"Stop what you are doing or I swear I'll kill you."

"So you are one of his; you can't want this, think of the murders, the children slaughtered for wanting to go to school ... we are prisoners of a terrorist. Why are you following him?"

"Let's go outside where your husband and child are about to die."

A fight ensues for several minutes, Genet is cut; she then produced a weapon of her own, a scalpel as she is being strangled.

"I am sorry," she says as she stabs the woman in the chest who wasn't expecting to lose the fight.

Schwartz is prepared but very nervous. Just then Genet exits the hospital and walks toward the three terrorists surrounded by several others, loyal followers. She all but ignores Mohammad and Sunrise. She approaches Warrior, not pleading with him this time to save husband and child and pulls off his mask and kisses him.

"Take the shot," David transmits the order.

"I'm shaking so much," came the reply, "I couldn't hit the broadside …"

"Calm yourself, hold your breath, take the shot … now," Preacher shouted.

He fired hitting Warrior and then his two generals, narrowly missing Genet. The other terrorists, surprised by the kill, coming from a distant hill, began to scatter. The team moved in to free the hostages, a gun battle ensued. Genet briefly hugs Mohammad as she runs to get the child and the doctor who follows with the parents of three small children.

"As I promised," she said, "the cure." She handed it to David. "The doctor is infected and as he recovers, will help the wounded and others infected. Find the children, they are being held captive, three of them."

"Head for that building," David said, "wait for us. Sunrise, Oaloff, go with them."

Several terrorists and sympathizers were killed, fingerprints were taken of the three using a flat laser pad along with a blood sample and picture of Warrior.

"This one's still alive," Oaloff said. "We'll take him with us."

David and the others took a thermal imaging device and went up and down several streets aided by the device to find the children. After searching several minutes, they were found. Gunfire was heard as the enemy closed in, then another was shot. Schwartz was still confident that he could frighten the enemy into believing there was a small army on that hill.

"Let's go," David said to the family; they met the others in the building where they were gathered. "We can't be extracted until we figure out an escape plan with a terrorist and two families in tow. We have classified information on terrorist plans to take over certain areas of Liberia spreading this new deadly disease on those they considered collateral damage while they, themselves would have been immunized by a cure," he told Base camp in case they didn't escape the enemy, "is a rescue chopper in route?"

"Negative ... we lost contact with the crew several hours ago ..." Just then David lost contact. They were surrounded and outnumbered as followers of Warrior, ever bent on revenge, continued the gun battle; their escape was blocked. David ordered those on the hill to remain there. Two were wounded as they returned fire. He then, looking for any escape, walked down a long corridor of the building where they had taken refuge needing a plan; he went upstairs checking for any food, ammunition, blankets if they escaped, medicines as well.

Adrian suddenly appears, David turns quickly to fire on an enemy but stops.

"Adrian, we need your help, I need your help ... we're all going to die. I'll submit ... just get us out of here."

He listens to David's plea, then, "Tell everyone to move downstairs, I'll create a diversion."

David quickly gathers everyone downstairs. "Follow me," he said, everyone was skeptical about escape, but followed; they couldn't see Adrian.

His diversion was a vision of hundreds of freedom fighters and military descending on the terrorists who were now distracted and frightened as they fired on the imaginary opposing forces and began firing on each other as confusion clouded their minds and believing David and his men with the families and a prisoner were still trapped.

"Go south," Adrian had told him; "those who would have rescued you are dead."

David then transmitted a message to his men on the hill – "Leave the truck, meet us going south these coordinates, enemy pursuing." He looked for Adrian but he was gone. Having completed their mission, they continued south, Adrian couldn't teleport them.

The families now understood the reality, that the extraction chopper had most likely been shot down and the crew was dead; they were on their own. They had evacuated so quickly that no warm clothing or blankets were brought. Energy bars and untreated water were the main sources of hydration and nourishment; there was an occasional meal of rat or snake cooked over a small fire and wild berries. They ate off the land as the Team relied on their survival skills to get themselves and their human cargo to safety. Pettigrew was credited with outstanding skills in surviving harsh conditions and in tracking resources for warmth, food and making fire.

The terrorist prisoner had been taunting them again and again; finally, he was gagged; he had threatened them and told them he would never be taken alive.

Four days later they found a helicopter behind a hill in a clearing surrounded by tall trees; there was no evidence of a crash as several bodies surrounded it. The enemy had killed the rescue crew and were guarding it. David suspected they weren't aware of their presence.

Oaloff came up with an idea to have the child cry while being held by Genet. "We can circle around behind and take them out before they fire a shot."

The enemy soldiers approached her and were about to take her and the child. Four of the men came behind the guards so quickly that none was able to fire their weapons. All three were killed; their comrades in the camp below weren't aware.

Sunrise began an inspection of the helicopter, an HH-60 Pave Hawk, as others examined the bodies of the dead crewmen; it would be a tight fit as they carried those that died.

"What brought it down was a damaged fuel line. I'll try to fix it; don't know if she'll fly or how long."

"All you can do is give us a chance," Preacher said.

He used whatever he could find aboard the helicopter; a tool box and medical kit would provide an answer, there were several tools and tubing.

An hour later, "Let's go home;" the bodies of the dead crew had been moved aboard, now the two families and finally David and his Team. It was almost dawn. "Pray."

The prisoner hadn't yielded answers; they had his fingerprints using a laser scanner. He made one last threat then was killed and left behind fearing what he might do once aboard. As the helicopter rose into the sky, Sunrise transmitted a message to home Base.

"We're coming – an enemy camp, these coordinates, twenty miles from first target appears to have no civilians from the air surveillance; they have stingers, one was fired, it shot past us, Pave Hawk is crippled, need escort."

"Copy that, head for Base, scrambling two F16's."

"Roger."

The enemy camp was destroyed and those aboard made it to an American base a hundred miles away. They gave the cure to be studied and replicated for the Liberian people who hadn't been immunized; everyone involved in the mission was screened for disease.

Lieutenant Mohammad and Genet expressed their thanks as did the other family. The men were debriefed. Troops, both Liberian and American took back the captured area held for two months by Warrior. Genet had given information on the terrorist plans for that region using the outdated transmitter the doctor had kept hidden. Warrior had been suspicious. The cyber skills of Ivan had been invaluable to the allies revealing further the terrorist plans and the funding sources.

Genet and Mohammad began a life in America, never to travel to the region again; she would have Warrior's child months later.

David and Mohammad had a private debriefing with the General as to what transpired and the reasoning for leaving a prisoner, one of the three terrorists, behind, executed. Colonel Blake was critical of this as he joined the meeting later.

"He presented a danger to us," Mohammad said, "and I killed him."

David asked for leniency, citing that the Lieutenant had made the mission possible.

The General listened, "This could end your career ... I'll handle it either way."

David contacted both Ana and Adrian.

"Everyone made it out ... both families are safe, no one contracted the disease that has killed hundreds and would been used on us and the freedom fighters, the ones that weren't an illusion."

"I'm glad for the outcome, meet with me aboard my ship 6:30, tomorrow evening; come unarmed."

"I gave my word, I'll be there."

He did see Ana first. "That's it on the missions most dangerous list." They made love; those words were what Ana wanted to hear.

"You said you're meeting with Adrian ... he might penalize you if you're late."

"You have no idea." David feared losing everything if he received an implant … to forget friendships, family, Ana – to forget love.

At 6:30 he arrived and entered Adrian's ship; there was no meeting that evening for the recruits.

"Adrian …"

"Were you about to ask me something? Are you ready for this?"

"I'm not sure. I have submitted myself to you as promised. Are you turning me into one of your sheep? This doesn't look like the machine used on the students."

"Because it isn't. Lie back."

"Restraints? This won't go well."

"I'm giving you something more powerful than an implant … a thirst for knowledge like no other … part of this are my changes to the laws of astrophysics. Your TA responsibilities will continue as you teach your class … this should keep you busy."

"The military?"

Adrian didn't answer as he pulled a visor over David's face and began the process of downloading his knowledge, not putting his entire spectrum into his mind, he wouldn't survive it. It was painful; an hour later the process was over. He woke up.

"How are you feeling?"

"Dizzy, mathematics seem to be clouding my mind."

"You're ready … tomorrow you'll proceed with Astrophysics 208 – calculating new discoveries using advanced math." He paused for a moment then, "Dr. Cordiero would be a good mate for you."

David was startled by the statement. "Can you read my thoughts without coming in contact with me?"

"Unfortunately no, but I do sense when you're in trouble needing my help."

The United States had been instrumental in carrying much needed food and medical supplies to Liberia, continuing to assist in driving out terror groups there assuming a lesser role than in Syria and Iraq. Their large cavernous C-17 Globemaster IIIs that brought the supplies were a welcome sight to a weary nation stressed by war and famine.

David had prepared for his class; his nights with Ana were complicated. While making love to her he would sometimes quote formulas.

"What's gotten into you?" She was excited about the new class even as she was competing with this new professor for his time. They would play a game, she would be his student and ask him questions, he would be the professor grading her performance. This helped to relieve his tension as he prepared. He had asked Adrian to tone down this thirst for knowledge.

"Ana has been understanding for now."

Adrian found this humorous, "I'll see what I can do."

"Another war has begun," David said as he watched it on HNN. The Syrian people are again massacred as their President- Dictator Bashar al-Asad is using barrel bombs against them as Russia continues to bomb their hospitals and medical supply convoys.

Adrian was well aware that turmoil on Earth continued as he made his monthly reports to the Vegan council. Earth's future hung in the balance.

One evening, three weeks later, Adrian and David attended a fund-raiser for the University to bring students from overseas to become part of a think tank as they received their education. Adrian's Think Tank had grown exponentially to fifty. Ana came with David. The Dean thought it was a worthwhile endeavor.

Other astrophysicists were asking Adrian questions and also pursued answers from David; several of the students attended and were asked about the textbooks written by Adrian that he was teaching along with theories from the old textbooks, many now fulfilled. A book was on display of the new math he created to prove his theories; he had been teaching it to David.

The Dean then introduced someone. "Professor Rodgers, this is Carlile Ironstone, entrepreneur, billionaire, fund-raiser, conservationist."

"I am an admirer of yours Professor." He and Carlile shook hands. "Excuse me, I feel a bit lightheaded."

Adrian introduced David; this is my protégé, Professor Eisen."

They shook hands. "Are you sharing the credit for your theories with him?"

"No," Adrian replied, "he is a quick study, however; these theories will take time to learn. Processing the information isn't easy by any means, but he will continue teaching my theories, two textbooks."

"I would like to attend one your lectures ... I'll call you soon to set up a date and time and of course discuss funds for bringing more students from various parts of the country as well as overseas."

Later, David questioned Adrian about what he learned from shaking hands with this eccentric billionaire.

"He believes I am an extraterrestrial or a human who has evolved on the evolutionary scale skipping ahead several generations ... this on the word of one of my implanted students. He plans on an abduction of sorts to find out. When he asked about you, his intent was to abduct you as well ... I convinced him otherwise."

"If you are abducted, can you be sure you'll escape them? They would use something to immobilize you."

"There is nothing I can be sure of when this happens. I must find out what his intentions are ... you'll have more to do at the University until I return."

"I can handle it." David was trying to be positive but his concerns for Adrian persisted. Adrian didn't disclose the name of the student, but he knew.

One evening, after class, Adrian was walking to his car. David had left earlier. Adrian hadn't been totally forthcoming with him; the abduction was happening as he knew it would a week later. David felt something was wrong and returned to the University to find him. He called the two men he trusted most, Pettigrew and Oaloff.

"Adrian is missing, I believe it was this Carlile Ironstone who came to the fund-raiser days ago, he abducted him."

"But why?" Oaloff asked.

Not mentioning the true reason why the abduction took place, he said, "Jealousy ... Adrian's discoveries along with the new math he developed to aid in those discoveries."

As they continued to look for clues, now at David's house, he entered Adrian's study, then as he sat he saw a paperweight, one of several he bought sitting on a desk. It appeared to move and communicate telepathically with him; he opened his mind to the communication not telling anyone.

"I know this is a guess, but Carlile Ironstone has a medium class sub; he would virtually be undetected taking Adrian anywhere."

Oaloff checked with the Navy and the departure of a sub registered to Carlile Industries.

"It departed several hours ago, 240 degrees west."

They continued to search his study. David took the paperweight. "It does move," he murmured to himself, Pettigrew was nearby.

"What moves? And what is all this?"

"The Professor says it's a learning tool." David knew firsthand what the machine could do, all the benefits, including a boosted IQ.

"You really have a lot of shit since he moved in."

"He's going to find someplace to live, but in the meantime …"

They surmised that Adrian was at sea in the Pacific headed for Carlile's private island, kidnapped, giving Carlile that lecture.

They rented a large seaplane packed with as much as they could carry to stage a scenario ahead of the sub. Oaloff attempted to pick up any sub signatures using sophisticated sonar and sub-bottom profiling motion analysis; now he chartered the course and speed.

In the meantime Carlile confronted Adrian, "You have been brought aboard as my guest … forgive the strong arm tactics. I have many questions that need answering and the lecture you'll be giving."

"I'll answer your questions as long as you bring me back to the University." For the first time on Earth, Adrian was feeling a new emotion, vulnerability.

"First, a tour is in order. This is my submarine, nuclear powered, 300 feet in length; let's get right to it … I study marine life, have for several years. My company harvests the oceans and as you can see, these scientists are working on ways to give back, to protect the environment. I call this ship the Explorer … who are you? Better yet, what are you? One of your students has ratted you out, saying you're an extraterrestrial, perhaps something else on the evolutionary scale; do you deny it? It was on Facebook."

"On Facebook? It's a rumor, students do that. I am flattered however."

"We'll test your DNA."

"Why?"

"Taylor showed me the implant in his neck, then there's the spaceship."

"What else has my student told you?"

"Several things. Let's have lunch then we'll see, I still want that lecture."

They had lunch and a special wine laced with an Isotope causing Adrian to succumb to the radiation emanating from the sub's reactor in an area close to sickbay; it rendered Adrian unconscious. He had hoped that the earlier communication with David through the paperweight would lead to a rescue.

"We must find him quickly," David said.

"Since we can track their course and speed, we'll fly ahead, say eight hundred miles and stage the scenario of a fishing boat adventure turned disaster as something rammed the boat, leaving only one survivor after it sank, only you," Pettigrew said.

"Sounds good. I could have been writing a documentary on those who fish the Pacific, the dangers or the profit … catching tuna? Cod? What?"

"Let's go with cod."

Oaloff began typing a fake ID presenting David as a reporter, also changing his biometrics information and fingerprint ID. "Your identity will match your story."

"Make me look like a survivor three days adrift."

"Rub your face with this and your arms, guaranteed to give you the ultimate sunburned look; bruising would help."

When they reached their goal of 800 miles ahead of the sub, they landed on the ocean; they had carried debris and had a life raft to stage the scenario. They poured fish debris on him, tore his shirt, Pettigrew punched him several times for a bruised look; his whiskers had grown somewhat. After throwing more debris in and around the raft, he was handed an ELT, several energy bars and water, he was ready.

"You two get gone, I owe you."

"We'll check on you, good luck." They flew out of the area.

Two days later, the sub found him and surfaced. David was dirty, tired, and smelled of fish.

"I'm Carlile Ironstone; you are aboard my mode of travel for sea journeys, the Explorer."

He responded to Carlile in English and hoped he didn't remember him, having met him at a fund-raiser. "Glad you and your sub came along when you did."

"What are you doing out here, so far from land?"

"I was documenting my experience aboard the Odessa, a 150-foot fishing boat, interviewing the crew as they worked and lived in all conditions; something rammed us hard ... by the way, I'm Gerald Wayne, of 'Fish and Wildlife Adventures Magazine'."

"There hasn't been any report about a boat called the Odessa being lost at sea."

"It might not have been reported yet."

"And you were the only survivor?"

"Yes, the ELT seems to have malfunctioned."

"Let's get you aboard, dry clothes, a meal."

Fingerprints were taken and biometrics scan; all confirmed his identity as Gerald Wayne.

"The shower is down the hall and a change of clothes," Carlile told him.

Afterward, he takes David on a tour of his 300-foot sub. "The reactor is in that room." Adrian was in an adjoining room where he was receiving a continuous minimal dose of radiation, preventing any possible escape. "This door will withstand and protect anyone viewing this masterpiece ... state-of-the-art technology."

"I'm certainly impressed ... I assume there is an infirmary."

"Sickbay? Nothing to see there." Carlile studied David for a moment ... "I have a strong feeling we have met before."

"I have one of those faces ... people think they know me."

David knew Adrian was there receiving doses of radiation in some manner and Carlile would eventually recognize him.

"Do you plan anymore documentaries on these fishing boats?"

"Honestly, after this, I don't know … I enjoy writing about things dealing with the oceans, but the reality is, there is always a danger."

There was a silence for a moment then, "Come with me, we'll surface for a while, take a look around."

It was evening, there was a full moon. David was taken with this; the stars, the constellations were very defined without pollution from cities obscuring the view. The air was fresh and invigorating. He respected Carlile from the beginning and what his life's mission was, preserving the ocean and the environment. He had to focus however, on planning an escape for Adrian and himself.

"You must be tired, Mr. Wayne. Before we take you to dry land, probably in two days, you'll experience our work in progress."

"Sounds interesting; looking forward to it."

That night, David attempted to search the sub. A guard was posted in the corridor, as the search was put on hold. Carlile was notified the next morning.

David went into cautious mode. Carlile made a suggestion at breakfast.

"Ready to get wet and see our progress?"

"I am scuba rated."

"I imagine you're rebreather rated as well … your training with the military included deep dives … your tattoo speaks volumes."

"I washed out … long story."

"I look forward to hearing it. We, on our quests, chose rebreathers for the longest dive times – they manage gas more efficiently, as you know, than open circuit scuba and are more complex. A fully closed rebreather completely recirculates the breathing gases; the semi-closed one expels a portion of the breathing gases as a part of its normal operation regardless of depth changes. Both types need to expel gases as you ascend to relieve pressure on the breathing loop as the gases expand. Long bottom times, little noise." Carlile continued, "The longest times in a dive are generally produced by fully-closed rebreathers as the Cis-Lunar or some of the Bio Marine Units and will allow a diver to stay underwater for over 8 hours on very little gas. Does that sound about right to you?"

"Sounds right," David replied.

"My son was into free diving. He died four years ago attempting to beat the record of 407 feet for 4 minutes and 34 seconds; he came close, but he drowned; died doing something he loved. He had become an underwater conservationist like myself and used both compressed air scuba and rebreathers. The record dive was 509 feet."

"Sorry to hear that," David said, "you must have been proud of him."

"Yes, even now ... we'll go deep, two of my crew, marine biologists will join us."

The sub had descended three hundred feet in order to secure samples. He showed David the signs of improvement, as in the growth of plankton and coral reefs, which were flourishing again. They had found an abundance of presumed extinct types of sharks over the Explorer's earlier journeys over several years; they had just found a type of ghost shark where life flourished much deeper. Carlile had explained the difference in shark communication, electrolocation, detecting electric fields using specialized electroreceptors to detect and locate the source of an electric field in its environment creating that electric field. The shark could then detect prey and avoid predators. He further defined echolocation used by dolphins not going as deep in the oceans. A Sensory Sonar System for finding prey determining size, shape, speed and distance and communication. Dolphin whistles were used for social interaction.

The food chain was returning to normal. There was an exhilaration that came with saving the environment; the tag and release program was very successful.

Two hours passed quickly; they decompressed and had dinner.

"What did you think as you were down there?" he asked David.

"More than I could have imagined." They watched the biologists studying the samples.

"I am looking for another species, something never seen before."

"What? Ocean?"

"Perhaps ... perhaps somewhere in an ocean, perhaps on land hiding out ... intelligent."

"Tell me more about this sub," David said. "Modern American attack subs as the Seawolf Class are estimated to have a test depth of

1600 feet with a collapse depth of 2400 feet. How does this compare to the Explorer?"

This question surprised Carlile; "About the same. We have two survival pods that could potentially prevent a disaster, loss of life."

"I will write about this."

"You should, you're interested in the ocean and conservation. I am also educating young people, one university at a time as I am invited to address the students and I raise funds for conservation studies."

During the night, David, avoiding security and any other encounters, searches for Adrian; he finds him incoherent. After sabotaging the reactor, stopping the sub, but not to explode, he takes Adrian three levels down. Holding a gun on the operator, they move toward the escape hatch. David has put on scuba tanks, not the rebreathers as time is short.

Suddenly, Carlile appears with two-armed security, "The Professor and his protégé, Colonel David Eisen."

"I'm asking you to allow us to leave … he's no threat to you or your work."

"If I say no?"

"Then I guess we'll both die trying."

"He's an alien or advanced on the evolutionary scale; which is it?"

"Neither; just a brilliant mathematician who is the world's foremost astrophysicist in my opinion."

"I don't believe you; you didn't sabotage the reactor to explode."

"We need you … the world needs you and other conservationists to save it; he's trying to do the same creating a Think Tank, bringing gifted minds into it to solve problems of pollution, discoveries in medicine, reaching out into the universe for answers."

Carlile listened, "Where were you planning to escape to when you both leave this ship … there is only ocean? We are below the depth to insure your survival." He hands David flippers, who continues to hold Adrian, keeping him standing up. "You both may leave now; if he is human, both of you will have the bends and die quite painfully … if he is extraterrestrial it would seem he could save you. I admire your loyalty … the sub stays at this depth none the less. I believe my theory is correct." Carlile doesn't mention Adrian's DNA. "I hope we meet again."

They enter the chamber to begin pressurization. David quickly instructs Adrian as the pressure in the chamber begins to equal the water pressure at escape depth.

"I'll take you as far as I can from the sub, but if you hear what I'm saying or thinking, get me to land as soon as possible and begin decompression." David now resorts to mental communication as the escape hatch opens. He repeated how long for decompression at the PSI level for the depth. "This will remove any chance that the nitrogen will have devastating consequences ... Don't destroy Carlile's ... I ...". He swims as far as he can from the sub, then exhausted, passes out. Adrian quickly comes to himself and heard every word.

Hours later David awakens and finds himself on a sandbar, a large one in the middle of the Pacific, miles from anywhere. Adrian is sitting emitting a signal for David's men to come; he didn't need an ELT.

"I trust the nitrogen is dissolved."

"Yes, and you?"

"Getting away from that reactor and the isotope I ingested is now out of my system ... you were correct, my safety was at great risk ... why did you save my life?"

"Carlile had you, your secrets and probably your origin ... perhaps using you as a bargaining chip against an invasion and ultimately causing our destruction by your people; he wouldn't intentionally start a war, but he couldn't or wouldn't see what research would produce if done on an extraterrestrial."

"I didn't destroy his sub until we discussed the matter."

"Carlile is and will be an asset to this planet starting with the oceans."

"He asked who I was ... I heard your reply; however, if he observed the escape, he knows the truth."

"I have to believe that wasting his life and research would be a mistake. As far as donating funds to bring students to this University and become part of the Think Tank, both of you are joined in that respect ... awkward!"

Carlile had observed the escape and was glad for the outcome.

"Why did you spare my life Adrian?"

"So that you and I can work out our differences. You have disrupted every meeting until lately, then the sabotage of facilities I've constructed, some affecting weather changes … you are, however, the constant in the equation, no implant, although I had considered it. I could see the world through your eyes."

"If you care about the human race, stop the devastating changes you've made in our weather … let's start there; are you still going to implant more students? Is there no other way for the variables?"

"Those decisions will come soon … and will you continue sabotage?"

David didn't answer. "And what about Carlile? It's your decision."

"I'll let him live … if he attempts this again on either one of us, I'll destroy him and his sub completely."

Pettigrew and Oaloff arrived in the seaplane. "Glad you both made it. How did you get here to a previously unknown sandbar in a thousand feet of water laid out like a small island? We passed over this area two days ago … we never saw it."

"I can't explain it," David said. "Adrian, you met Pettigrew and Oaloff at a gathering at my house months ago; they helped in your rescue."

Adrian attempted to shake hands, David prevented him from doing so, protecting both from having their minds read.

"We owe you our thanks," he said.

"You both didn't decompress," Oaloff said.

"The sub was above decompression level," David replied.

There was silence as both Pettigrew and Oaloff knew better. They wanted more answers about the kidnapping; they weren't satisfied that Carlile had plans to steal Adrian's work – his theories concerning astrophysics and the math he developed to prove them.

Once they reached home again they prepared for their classes; the General met with David, Pettigrew and Oaloff.

"Chasing a sub, rescuing the Professor at the risk of your lives …" the General wasn't pleased.

"Carlile Ironstone had kidnapped him intending to steal his work to be used as he saw fit, we suspect for producing weapons. Adrian doesn't build weapons, so he was to be terminated if he didn't cooperate."

"Was Carlile terminated or anyone aboard?"

"No Sir, no way to save the Professor and leave the sub if it erupted into a gun fight."

"This was an unauthorized mission."

"Yes sir … I take full responsibility." David knew the severity of his actions.

"I am to be informed of any and all missions as I will authorize them, do I make myself clear?"

"Yes Sir."

"There won't be disciplinary action … dismissed," he said.

They were relieved. Blake wasn't in on this meeting as the General ordered. This frustrated him feeling he was being pushed out.

David met with Ana, she knew the mission was a success, just not everything; he felt frustrated that everything was a half-truth since meeting Adrian, guarding the truth about his missions by downplaying the dangers. He was given more time in the machine.

Taylor, Adrian's student confessed, having revealed that he was probably extraterrestrial to Carlile; he was later found dead, a heart attack it was surmised. Taylor had murdered Seth who had been helping David discover what Adrian had been up to as he established certain devices to control the weather. The student was dangerous and mentally off even before the implant and the murder; he was responsible for killing Rex, David's dog as he spied on him, buried with honors for having served.

Both Adrian and David were quickly grading papers, catching up after their ordeal with Carlile. David fought exhaustion.

Days later, Colonel Blake confronted Ana demanding to be informed and to read the reports on David's mental state and progress after the Vietnam mission. She refused his earlier advances and gifts, all to lure her away from David and into giving him anything he asked for; she didn't tell anyone, not even David; weeks passed.

Then a call. David's former commander and friend Costanza died. He told the men, most of whom had served under him as well. When he retired five years earlier, David became his successor. He was given a brief funeral in Peru, closed casket. The Team attended as did General Gonzales and others he befriended over the years of the General's family and army. Costanza was flown back to California where he received a burial with honors in the National Veterans Cemetery near Los Angeles. General Stevens officiated paying respect to this highly decorated Army Ranger.

David visited that cemetery weeks later. He was there for over an hour, emotionally torn over this loss and pouring out his feelings about Ana and the missions, his duty to his country and how he might lose her if he didn't stop the missions.

Someone in the distance was watching and began walking in his direction and stood behind him. "I've been keeping an eye on you," a man in a hoodie said.

David turned and in disbelief, "How can this be – that you're alive? You died."

"Close; Le Mur's men were closing in, we would be overrun within a week. Gonzales and his soldiers would be executed if they didn't join him, 'no opposition and live', he said. Gonzales shook my hand as he said, 'Several will die, you must leave now.' Then my death was orchestrated. Gonzales gave me a half-million US to start a life somewhere."

"Who did we bury?"

"I'm not sure; I didn't ask but I took his advice, left the country with Sarah, his cousin and her two kids … you met her on your last visit. We made our way to Mexico, new passports, new lives. We have since moved to an island. I'm out of the war business; occasionally I assassinate a bad guy. I like the fishing, especially expeditions … don't tell anyone, that includes the Team and anyone else you know … it could cause problems."

"I won't … you're the inspiration I needed Costanza."

"Marry her … take care of yourself … I'll be in touch." They shook hands and then he was gone.

A courier delivered a package to Ana's office two days later. David had a meeting with the General and his men that afternoon. She discussed the package with her secretary.

"It obviously is from David but do I open it now?"

She called him.

"I'm still at the Base, be there soon."

"I got the most mysterious package today ... tell me what it is ... can I open it now?" she laughed.

"I didn't send it ... what does it look like?"

"Silver box, red ribbon tied in a bow, about 5" x 5"."

"I'm on my way don't ..." Just then her phone went dead. David was frantic as he left quickly and called 911 with her address. "Suspicious package, might be a bomb." He met the police at her office; he entered the room, the box had been opened. Ana quickly hugged him, she was frightened, the box contained C-4 and a timer. The timer had been disconnected before being delivered the police said.

"You're lucky to be alive as well as your staff – someone was going to make sure this was your last day or frighten you," an officer told her. Just then David received a call, it was Le Mur, he took the call in an adjoining room.

"You son-of-a-bitch ... now you're after her?"

"Listen carefully ... I saved her life, she has enemies as you do; we thought it strange that package came from a sworn enemy of yours. My bomb and demolitions expert intercepted it, diffused it and sent it on. Think of her safety as well and consider this a wedding gift."

David didn't have a chance to reply or know who the real enemy was. Ana suspected.

There were discussions about Earth's future. Adrian and David had come to respect each other; he pressured Adrian to shut down a power disrupter he had designed, which was in place to cause a massive power outage if needed; a disruption in the state's major power source was part of his plan to subdue the human race if necessary, going state to state.

"I need your help to shut it down," David said, "some flexibility."

"You and two of your men have sustained injuries from previous sabotage ... nevertheless, I will do as you ask."

"These drastic weather changes are still occurring."

"I haven't caused all of this; you humans bear the responsibility for most of it. I will help the situation as I can."

"The General has authorized a mission to find who tried to have me and my Team executed by sabotaging our missions; minimal danger."

"There is always danger in your missions; how long?"

David approximated the time needed and got Ben to substitute as TA for Adrian until he returned. He discussed with the General what he had to do.

"Get a verbal recording of the confessions as well as affidavits from Colonel Mihn and Private Bentley to expunge the records of all who went on the ill-fated mission to Vietnam. You'll be working this one alone; it comes from the top in case things go south, but I know you're resourceful; they're leaning on me on this one." The General was concerned.

He understood and now begins his search for the Colonel using any and all resources at the Base working to track him down. Days went by but he found him in Cuba at a bar he frequented. David was armed, he doesn't display his weapon as he moves closer to his sworn enemy.

"Are you here to kill me Colonel David?" Mihn appeared tired and miserable drinking to forget past sins. He takes another drink. "Come sit."

He hesitates, then, "No, I'm not here to kill you … I want to talk."

"Can I buy you a drink?"

"American beer will do."

"We are witnessing history in Cuba after fifty years. The American Embassy is again open; people can now travel freely here … I have lived here long enough to make it my home … I always knew you would find me, I let you live, two of your men were killed before I could intervene … I regret this … that young overzealous" … referring to his Lieutenant Mao; "I put a bullet in his head, he tried to kill me."

"Who was giving you information, who sabotaged our mission?"

"The one who paid me to execute you and your men … I believe you work with him on missions, a Colonel Blake Barnard; the extraction transmission was received but blocked ... he blocked it so I would execute all of you before the rescue; he promised me anything to not see your face again, it was a great sum of money. I have no army now. I have written this for you and other documents to prove sabotage at the hands of Colonel Blake; you and your men will be exonerated and this recording of our conversation confirms everything. You are a true warrior and your men are loyal."

David held the documentation and verbal confessions on his phone; he stood up to leave the man he hated for so long and hating him no more, not wanting to kill him but not shaking his hand.

"God bless your house Colonel," he said in Vietnamese. This surprised David and he returned a similar blessing in English.

He took time to view the Embassy and other parts of Cuba before returning home, watching history unfold as diplomatic relations were restored.

He returned home a day later; he put this information in a vault in a separate storage facility. He didn't go to the Base but met with his men at home before tracking Private Bentley. "As you know this is part two of an authorized mission. I'll again be working alone as the General is unauthorized to allow the manpower. We are being judged already as guilty and it seems this is part of it. Colonel Mihn was forthcoming with the information ... Colonel Blake orchestrated our failure. I have a vault, not on Base, not here. When I return, hopefully the Private will have substantiated our story. Thanks for the intel and hours put in tracking both the Colonel and Private Bentley. If you attempt to assist me, you could be in for a court-martial ... wish me luck."

The men were uneasy about this and discussed what they might do.

David prepared to find the next witness now living in Pennsylvania Amish country; the radio operator Private Al Bentley had received the original extraction signal on Base. David knew Colonel Blake would try to find the Private or already had. He found him after four days of searching at a small Amish church.

"My wife and child are in danger – he found me a month ago, a message was left for me in my coat pocket by someone I assumed worked for him."

"Why not go the military for protection? I don't see you as Amish," David's attempt to lighten the mood.

"You won't see me as anything if he knows I talked to you."

"So this person who left you the note could have followed you here, blended in, gotten to know you and your family with orders to kill you if you talked. Tell me about the signal sent for rescue."

"You can call me Will Hutchins." He told David everything. The confession was documented, an affidavit was signed and recorded by cell phone, stating that Colonel Blake ordered him to ignore a transmission signal sent by two of David's men causing their deaths and subsequent torture for six weeks for those imprisoned. This gave David the proof he needed.

Private Bentley introduced him to his family and showed what life was like living as a farmer and craftsman in a different culture and environment. David knew he should leave but he felt the family was in danger.

"He mustn't see you here … and I regret the pain I caused you and your Team."

"It wasn't your fault."

"I kept telling myself that. I married an Amish woman, a widow and adopted her son soon after … I could be happy here."

They had a meal together that evening. "Is this how the Amish treat visitors?" David complimented her, "A sumptuous meal." Nora smiled. "This appeals to me …"

"That's not the only reason I married her," he said and held her hand. David stayed the night. He watched the night sky, the fresh air was invigorating.

Later, before dawn, he heard someone exit the house and two were heard talking. The one who left returned a few minutes later as it was approaching daybreak. David followed Bentley to the barn and was shown how a typical Amish day started. They took a carriage into town, buying supplies, groceries and introducing David as an old friend. This was in his plan to lure the threat out in the open and away from Bentley and the family.

"Who were you talking to early this morning?"

"Just another farmer like myself; we help each other, he runs a market."

Later, he found the two of them in the barn, they were arguing. David confronts the stranger.

"So you're the one to tie up loose ends ... do you work for Colonel Blake?"

"Where are the documents, the affidavits?" the stranger asked angrily.

"What are you talking about? You work for Colonel Blake."

"Kill him," he told Bentley.

"It's you." Bentley was shocked. "We worked together, bought our groceries from your market; you're in our church family, you held my son, enjoyed meals with us ... is your real name Steil?"

"It doesn't matter now ... you kill the Colonel."

The click of the gun was heard.

"How long have you known Colonel Blake?" David asked.

"You mean Colonel Barnard ... long enough."

"What happens when the Private kills me? Do you kill him, his family?"

"Does it matter?"

"Listen to me Bentley, he's going to make you take the fall for this and kill any witnesses."

"Kill him now, head shot."

"Get on your knees Colonel." David complies. Bentley is shaking as he holds the gun. Suddenly, out of the dark corner of the barn, someone takes a few steps then takes a shovel to the man holding a gun on Bentley killing him.

"Oaloff?"

"That would be me. I suspect he's dead, head bashed in ... Pettigrew and Vinnie are here, two trucks. Sunrise is waiting at a rendezvous point; we changed your plan a bit, figured you might need the help."

"How right you were."

Bentley lowered the gun as he was given instructions.

"You can't stay here, not if you want to live ... pack quickly, the two trucks," Oaloff told him.

"We split up heading for the rendezvous point in thirty," David said.

Several miles down the road there was a barrage of gunfire as they were pursued; they returned fire as they took each truck on a different route eventually stopping their pursuits and ending up at an extraction point – safe for the moment as they abandoned their vehicles and climbed aboard an awaiting chopper. They flew the family to a safe house in California until the documents were presented to the General; the family was protected by two agents.

David now had the proof he needed. Once they left, having delivered Private Bentley and his family to an undisclosed location, they flew back to Base. They knew they could be disciplined for assisting David on his mission, but this was of out of their control and it was their choice.

He then left for home after collecting the information from a vault adding to Private Bentley's confession, documentation and affidavit. He had an ominous feeling that he might not see Ana again or the General; he called a courier to deliver the proof, including a confession, hand written, from himself. If he tried to deliver this, Blake could potentially stop him with devastating consequences. He hoped he wouldn't intercept the delivery, he had allies everywhere and would stop David from implicating him and vindicating the Team, even resorting to murder; he hadn't slept in hours but pushed himself.

David had called Ana and would see her that evening at a favorite restaurant. He purchased a ring and flowers and would propose over dinner; no mention was made of Blake's treachery and vindictiveness. He would tell her how the mission went.

With the ring and flowers in the front seat, he stressed over how he would propose to her; it was dusk. Suddenly he was hit from behind by a truck, then two more times as a car pulled up to his left side and fired. Bullet proof glass saved him as the car forced him off the road onto an unfinished stretch of highway. He stopped, quickly evaluated the situation and exited his truck. With any route of escape blocked, he and three men approached each other, his pistol was tucked inside his pant leg – his large knife was now in hand.

"You fellows ran me off the road … want to tell me why?"

One laughed, "You're gonna wish you'd never met us when this is over – you suffer, then die."

"Blake must have sent you boys … I hope he paid you; no accents … are you local talent?"

"Give us the information."

"What information?" He never mentioned a courier.

"North Vietnam, anything, everything."

"I don't have it, certainly not here." He saw two moving in on him with a can of gasoline and a lighter. "He has to film this?" David said as he looked at a third moving in from behind. His instinct for survival was kicking in.

"Tell us where and your death will be a quick one."

"Somehow I doubt that." David went for his pistol while fighting ensued – unable to reach it in time he fought hand to hand using his formidable knife. Each one was wounded early on as fighting intensified. He stabbed one. "Two left," he said has he held his abdomen, bleeding from a deep cut. Martial arts put everyone on an equal footing. David was a third degree Black Belt.

"You must be bleeding badly," one said, "loosing strength."

Suddenly David delivered a kick to the one who mocked him, breaking his neck and stabbed the third. He fell then steadied himself as he was bleeding out. He reached his truck and drove quickly to a hospital almost passing out, honking his horn, swerving to miss crashing into other cars. He called 911 but didn't sound coherent, unable to tell who his attackers were or where he was located. He made it to emergency, drove up the steps, opened the door and fell out on the concrete.

An hour passed, several were called. Adrian arrived before being called sensing David was in trouble, a life and death struggle. Several were standing in the hall, the General was there with the men.

Ana was in her office preparing to meet David. Blake heard her phone ring; she had turned off all lights but a desk lamp unaware that Blake was there. Before she could answer it he came from behind shoving her to the floor; she was in shock seeing him and fought as he continued his assault.

"I want those profiles on Colonel Elsen."

"You're not getting them."

"I'll make you get them." He tore her clothes as he beat her; she screamed and continued to fight back as he tried to violate her. "You'll never see him again."

A maintenance man heard her screams and entered, Blake ran out the door, face covered.

"Are you all right Dr. Cordiero?"

"I will be thanks to you … did you see his face?"

"No, I didn't."

"Don't report this."

"But …"

"I'm ok … he won't be back." She checked her phone and the message, quickly changed clothes and headed for the hospital.

The General questioned the doctor extensively; the police were notified and had briefed him on the events that transpired, finding three men, all dead, all had weapons.

Ana arrived, Adrian sat by her and held her hand. She was severely traumatized and was about to pass out; she had bruising.

"I fell … I'm fine." She couldn't stand due to weakness. Two of her co-workers were sitting with her for moral support in an open area facing the hall. As Adrian held her hand she began to cry as the General talked with her and handed her the ring and flowers. Adrian read her thoughts and as he did so he never felt emotion like this so strong between two people and one so devastated; he realized she had been attacked. The General heard the men talking, he joined the conversation.

"We know it was Colonel Blake," one told him … "he has fixated on destroying him somehow, even to sabotaging our missions."

They discussed the police report and the papers that would have exonerated them if found.

David briefly opened his eyes, unable to talk due to a breathing tube, saw Adrian standing there by his bedside, his eyes, his thoughts said, "Don't bring me back," then closed his eyes.

"Crash cart," the doctor yelled, "he's flat-lined;" three entered the room, Adrian stayed refusing to leave. He locked the doors as the others were distracted walking over to the bed when David was pronounced dead, then taking his hand he briefly changed form emitting an energy boost twice.

Moments later, "We're getting a heartbeat," a nurse shouted.

The confounded staff saw this but were unable to process what they had just witnessed. Adrian congratulated them and made them remember events that didn't include him, believing they had saved David. The door was opened again; everyone for the moment felt relieved.

"His vitals are returning to normal, he might just make it," the doctor said; "he'll be kept in a medically induced coma for now."

Blake briefly made an entrance but was blocked from the area by David's men. Ana wasn't aware he was there. The General was in the hall as he gave encouragement and ordered Blake to leave for his safety.

The next day the courier arrived at the General's office. Blake wasn't aware that a parcel had already been delivered before he arrived. The General began reading the documentation as well as listening to the audio-video accounts on one of David's I-phones; there was another document with the others, a confession from David:

["General, I leave you this confession, I might not have another chance. Six years earlier I was on a mission led by Colonel Blake to Mogadishu. Commander Costanza had been wounded and Colonel Blake was ordered to lead this mission. There were pockets of Al— Shabbab terrorists to extinguish and the good guys, who needed our help, putting themselves on the line to help us. There were those who infiltrated those villagers who were on our side; several were promised a new start somewhere. Colonel Blake backed out of the deal when we were faced with several weeks of an extended stay to find and weed out the enemy. He discussed a plan, killing the villagers, as well as a few infiltrators to be sure there was no more threat. We were told to gather them into a large barn; the three of us protested as we were given orders to execute them. Blake threatened us to follow orders. I never fired on these people, nor did I try to stop it … thirty died. Blake made it clear if I told anyone, he would make sure I would be stripped of my rank as Major and you, General, would take the fall for this mission and probably dishonorably discharged; he threatened all of us with similar fates.

This has weighed on me for six-years and what he's capable of. I don't have a clear conscience but I did not participate in the massacre. I almost killed him to stop it. I don't know if I've been chasing a bullet all this time, taking the Team on suicide missions at times; it seems to me to be a vindication of sorts. The two from our unit who disagreed with Colonel Blake and unwillingly participated in the massacre, died months later of mysterious causes.

Be aware of his treachery; you have been a special mentor to me – Colonel David."]

The General called in Colonel Blake for a meeting. He saw the parcel and its contents on the General's desk. Blake was about to kill him and take the evidence when an MP stepped into the room.

"This information I received today clears Colonel Eisen and his men of the failed mission to Vietnam and includes testimony of sabotage on your part of dismissing an extraction transmission, alerting and paying the enemy to murder two UN inspectors along with Colonel Eisen and his men. Other acts on your part will be investigated as well as the Mogadishu incident ... I'm promoting Lieutenant Colonel Eisen to Colonel; he and his men will receive purple hearts for heroism. You have 24-hours to make arrangements and return here to be incarcerated awaiting court martial proceedings; if Colonel Eisen dies, you'll be indicted for his murder."

"Promote him to full Colonel status? You've lost your mind," Blake said.

"You are dismissed Colonel, get him out of here," he told the MPs. Blake was furious.

A week later, Ana took David to recover at her house. She hired help as needed. Adrian kept in contact giving her another one of the infamous paperweights. He could then monitor David's progress and hers concerning his recovery and her safety. Friends came to be supportive and be of assistance. The men took turns watching as protectors for both. Colonel Blake had escaped after shooting both MPs; both would recover; the General then added his own security protection for Ana and David.

David had begun to come around but slept almost continually; he wasn't entirely aware yet of the circumstances of his injuries. The General made several visits.

One afternoon Adrian visited Ana and as always checked on David's progress. She began to tell him what was in her heart. "I feel very close to you ... David always called you his good friend."

"I'm flattered." Adrian wasn't expecting this, especially when David was angry with him and used other words as 'Bastard'.

"I fixed lunch for us, hope you like it ... I don't know if he survives this and I think he will, will he be the same as he was?"

"I believe he will."

"I lost my husband five years ago from an IED in Iraq on one of those dangerous missions ... I'm still not over it." She showed Adrian the ring David gave her. "Of all things I fell in love again with a man who had dangerous missions ... some call them suicide missions; his license plate has the word AMMO on it ... so I knew the dangers and risks that came with the job – that came with the man. I told him I couldn't marry him if he continued the high risk ones."

"When he recovers, he'll have a job with me as TA and continue to teach his class as a professor."

"That's just it, he wants both ... to stay with the military planning the missions, just not participating in them directly and his class ... you've had quite an influence on him."

In a few moments Adrian asked her, "Is war a necessity in your opinion?"

This question she answered carefully. "I am basically a pacifist, but there are reasons for war; there are those who would suppress others who are free or fighting to be free – not submission or blind obedience. The human race has thrived where there is freedom ... and freedom comes at a price; to not be free is death for us. Someday, perhaps we won't need war and casualties will be a thing of the past."

Adrian took all of this very seriously; he checked on David before he left giving him a smaller burst of energy and the words, "Your students are waiting for you and I need my TA. When you are able, meet me at Silas Road, there is much to discuss."

Ana continued to work from home. She would lie in bed with him, reading to him a favorite novel to stimulate his mind. He couldn't yet steady a razor, she assisted and cut his hair as well.

The men would watch football with David; he just sat with anyone visiting until the game was over saying very little. They were glad just to see him awake but remained concerned; he had lost weight.

Three weeks passed then he began an exercise regiment with an Army therapist. He had begun to walk down the hall without assistance, his strength went quickly, he fell at times, the frustration was evident. Ana would just sit on the floor beside him; even frustrated, he laughed, she would laugh, they kissed.

A special morning came. He ate breakfast, showered and shaved. Ana inspected and gave the thumbs up.

"I'm back," he told her. "I'll be gone for an hour ... Silas Road ... I want to see the ocean, then I'm headed back." He held her close for a few moments and kissed her. She reluctantly let him go.

He arrived before Adrian and sat on the hood of his car listening to the sounds of the ocean as it beat against the rocks; seagulls flew above. Adrian arrived and was standing behind him.

"You've got to teach me how to teleport."

"I was wondering when my TA would return ... your class needs you."

"What did you not understand about not bringing me back?"

"I understood ... I chose not to agree to your wish. Ana was alone, vulnerable. A man you call Colonel Blake violated her, so if you died, she was defenseless; this happened the night you were attacked."

David registered shock and disbelief as he held a hand to his mouth. "Did he rape her?"

"Fortunately he didn't complete the rape; she fought him off until help arrived. Understand this David, there are those who need you, who depend on you. I don't always agree with your methods to save the world. You were always the constant in this."

"But what meaning does it have if you won't listen, turn us into sheep or incinerate the planet?"

"There were two possibilities, now there is a third; the third choice is yours."

"What is it?"

"Find out when you return to class."

Then Adrian left. David drove back to Ana's. They discussed the night of the violation; she cried, he held her.

"Who told you this?"

"Does it matter who told me? I wasn't there for you."

"How could you have been? You were dying ... I felt myself dying with you."

They both cried, he made love to her.

"Blake has caused enough problems in this world."

"He wanted to see the progress reports on you and your men. I refused, he became angry and was in my office waiting when the attack happened."

"I sent a parcel by courier to be delivered personally to the General; the attack happened the night before he received it ... evidence clearing me and the team in the Vietnam mission and accusing him of sabotage on this mission and others. You once told me I was chasing a bullet ... you were right. I included a confession about not stopping a massacre of friendly villagers in Mogadishu years earlier. Terrorists, we know, had infiltrated these villagers who had been promised a new life in America for helping us. I didn't participate in their murders which Blake initiated; he outranked me ... he will pay for what he's done." David became emotional. "There were threats made against us and the General's future if we revealed the truth ... he almost terminated the General who confronted him with the evidence in the parcel; luckily there was an MP close by. Blake was escorted home for 24-hours to collect any pertinent papers for his defense regarding a court martial; he escaped the two MPs and fled, so he's out there somewhere, maybe watching us. The General was satisfied that we were being looked after ... I'm sure he has those of his own posted close by as well."

David and his Team had been exonerated and were now decorated for their service and bravery; all received purple hearts, two were elevated in rank. David was made a full Colonel. Ninety percent of their missions were successful it was stated in the General's report.

"Proud of you David," the General whispered as he penned his new rank to his uniform and saluted him. Oaloff was later to command the Team. A hundred attended the ceremony. Adrian was sitting with Ana; it was locally televised. The University students were given time to watch a brief recap of the ceremony on news. Colonel Blake also watched the news; his anger boiled. David would step down as Special Ops Commander as he appointed Oaloff as successor. He would, however, plan the missions with him and the Team involved. The General always participated in the planning.

"There is a last mission to take down Colonel Blake before I step down."

"Let's do it," Oaloff said.

David began working with Adrian on the third possibility for Earth and the survival of the human race as an evolutionary step would occur at some point where there would be understanding between the races and preservation of Earth would become a focal point, not war and not poisoning the environment.

Adrian stopped the implant procedures and used the meetings to discuss ways not to destroy, but to preserve. David was at every meeting making suggestions, no disruptions, no sabotage.

"I have discussed this with my people," he told David. "Now I must return to my world and present the facts to convince them, the Vegan Council, that humanity is no threat; but even as their leader, they could all come against me and destroy your world. David, I need your help. If you travel there with me, the chances are better ... you might not survive the trip however."

David was thinking this through, carefully considering Adrian's desperation. "How long?"

"The ship converts into light, warp twelve, a month to get there, a month to return, if we are allowed to leave."

"The General won't go for anyone to be on personal leave for two months. What now?"

"We'll be on a two-month trip but reverse relativity will cause it to seem like we've been gone three days; why don't you ask the General for three days personal leave? We leave tomorrow evening."

"I'll call Ana, Oaloff and Pettigrew to meet me tomorrow night at Villa Road and give them instructions. I trust them to tell no one."

"What I've told the Dean is that we're going on a recruiting trip to London."

Later, David called the General and got the ok. He met with Ana, Oaloff brought her, Pettigrew arrived soon after; they were in disbelief seeing him walk out of the ocean.

"Adrian and I are going on a mission which concerns the human race. As secrets go, keep this one from the others ... he is an extraterrestrial."

"And we were worried about you going solo," Pettigrew quipped.

"David, are you joking?" Ana said.

"Look out for each other ... I'm part of a negotiation with Adrian's world, Vega. The Vegan Council seems determined to meet a human and discuss our future. Adrian is on our side; he is head of the council. We'll be gone for two months, but with reverse relativity, it will be only three days here on Earth," he handed Ana the car keys.

"Colonel, you have our word, Ana will be protected ... this is hard to believe ... what's your true mission when you get there?" Oaloff asked.

"To have them believe that the human race should be allowed to survive.

He kissed Ana and shook hands with his two closest friends. "Be here in three days, late evening. Move to higher ground by those rocks ... takeoff will be spectacular."

"If something goes wrong?" as she looked in his eyes.

"It won't." He returned to the waterway. Several minutes passed as he dressed for the trip, a uniform designed for him. Suddenly lightening flashed across a clear sky then a sound like thunder as the ship rose above the ocean and terrifying energy emanated from the ship's engines.

"It's saucer shaped," Oaloff yelled, "and to think I didn't believe him."

"David, come back to me," Ana whispered.

The ship converted into light about to begin its journey.

"Before I'm put in stasis, show me those newly discovered planets in case we don't make it back."

"A small detour ... yes."

David was amazed as they first went in the opposite direction past each known planet and those two recently discovered, each a billion miles or more from Pluto.

"They're going to have to grant Pluto full planet status again when they see what we are seeing … and ice and salt water on Mars. They could plan colonization … a scientist by the name of Dr. Hoffman detected water in 2008."

"We're reversing course now … this stasis chamber should be sufficient."

David entered, he slept.

A month later they reached Vega. David was retrofitted with a small breathing apparatus; two attendants met them both, having the appearance of Adrian's form, that of white energy. They were taken to the Council Chamber where six others were anxious to have Adrian return and meet the first human they had ever seen; they spoke in their native tongue, then in English."

"Welcome back Counselor Mafusa," one said, "and to you Earthling."

"This is Colonel David Eisen … he has become important to me and is a most crucial piece of the human puzzle; he has my respect as a friend and a problem solver. I will protect him at all costs."

David was moved by what he heard.

Both sat as the six on the Council were seated around a large semicircular table facing them.

"We are concerned that Earth is becoming a danger to us," a feminine voice said … "would you agree?"

Adrian countered, "Human beings aren't children, they're not to be treated as such. We've had wars on Vega, we brokered peace, we are better for it; as far as a danger to us … no."

"War as a solution?" another asked him.

"Sometimes wars must occur to usher in the next step in evolution."

"We would hear you David … a man of war."

"Adrian, I know him by this name, and I don't always agree. Our differences have us working together. You are correct that I am a man of war. I fight against those who are, by their very nature, oppressing people who value freedom above all else. They are destructive in their thoughts, always against those who cannot help themselves; war is necessary to even the odds. If you study humankind from the beginning, we have learned to negotiate peace in the midst of tragic unrest."

One of the Council, masculine, stood up and brought a book to David; he then reads from it: "'Dangerous, a threat to be investigated, submission or destruction of their world. I cannot allow Colonel Eisen to sabotage my efforts.' Later he writes, 'I will not allow him to die; there is a third solution. I am teaching him about the universe, he is teaching me about his world.' Key thoughts for your world; Adrian transmitted these thoughts to us over time ... this speaks highly of your species."

Another said, "Define the third solution; would you be monitoring them?"

"I would, working with David. I would appear human as before."

"This then is a new thing you are attempting."

"I would be there implementing new ideas for peace, guiding them into the next stage of their existence; this will take time."

"David?"

"I agree; not turning us into sheep ... docile creatures with a herd mentality."

"How long would you be gone Adrian? What would you ask of the Council?"

"To remain Chief of Council in absentia; as far as length of time, undetermined."

"So you have touched this one saving his life; does he have an implant?"

"Is he changed?" another asked.

"No, and I expect no changes." Adrian knew if David was changed, he wouldn't be allowed to leave Vega.

"We will discuss this matter and render our decision, but first ..." All six Council members stood up and surrounded David, touching him, reading his thoughts, he began to hyperventilate.

"Calm yourself David, you won't be harmed," Adrian said, ready to intervene if necessary; he passed out.

An hour later he awakened. "The decision?"

"They agreed to it; you'll feel drained for several hours ... their intent wasn't to harm you as they based their decision on your thoughts and actions as well as your responses to their questions and my thoughts concerning you."

They were fed; food was unlike anything he had tasted before, more of a vegetable nature; there was water, not unlike Earth's water, it weighed in much lighter; gravity was less than that of Earth. The atmosphere had a reddish glow due to frequent dust storms in some areas. Three small moons orbited Vega which orbited a large white sun. Besides vegetation, there were fruit groves in the areas where there was moisture and trees. Animals generally looked menacing when being pursued, most were small, four footed, not usually a food source. Adrian was giving David a short tour even showing him buildings, metal curved structures generally dome shaped; an overview of the planet in a space shuttle. The UV rays from the sun were intense but necessary.

"War? Family?"

"We have learned from war ... family, complicated to describe ... I'll tell you about it sometime. I have no offspring, but as we live much longer than human beings, most wait until late in life to procreate."

Last of all he showed David the Council Chamber's ancient records on other civilizations as well as their own beginning. "Each species of beings encountered on other worlds, were carefully monitored as were Earthlings and their development. Some of the species were wiped out if seen as dangerous and destructive; each one of those books represents every civilization discovered.

This bothered David, "So Vegans are the police of the universe."

"Putting things in order," Adrian replied. "This has happened for millennia. We can leave now; their fears were that you could fall into the wrong hands once we returned."

"Carlile?"

"Perhaps worse."

Another from the Council spoke as they were escorted to Adrian's ship. "This has enlightened us to meet you David; regular progress reports must be made ... work together on this. Now we leave you for your journey home."

"We dodged a bullet," David said once aboard ship.

"Several."

Two months had passed, they returned creating an electrical storm to cover the presence of a space ship; it was evening. Ana, Pettigrew and Oaloff were waiting. Adrian's ship had scanned where Colonel Blake was, hiding an arsenal he was building, before burrowing itself again in the ocean. They welcomed Adrian with a new respect of being an extraterrestrial who made himself an advocate to protect Earth and as David's friend who no longer regarded him as the enemy.

"Three days," Ana said as she also welcomed Adrian, she kissed David, hugging him. "But you both were gone two months ... doesn't this go against relativity as we know it?"

"Yes it does and we'll explain; so much to tell you. Adrian's ship has pinpointed where Blake is ... Guadalupe Island."

"What's our next move?" Oaloff asked, "and glad you're back;" they shook hands.

Pettigrew hugged him, looked at Adrian, "I would have never figured you for an extraterrestrial, but I'm glad you're on our side."

"I will help as needed."

"You already have," Oaloff said.

Ana gave Adrian a hug, "Thank you."

"For what?"

"Bringing him back, listening."

The next day the Team met with the General. "Do you trust your intel?"

"He's building an arsenal," Oaloff said, "we have satellite confirmation."

"To what end?"

"Perhaps turning terrorist," Ivan said ... "he's sick."

David made a bold suggestion, "Let's give him what he wants, weapons and me." Just then David got a call.

"Better get on the move, Guadalupe Island; he is there now for about two more days to complete an arms deal."

"Le Mur?"

"It's probably a trap and obviously he wants you as well ... I can take him out but then where is your revenge ... no satisfaction there.

Take him out literally, no trial, no fuss … if you don't, he'll destroy everything you hold dear; that includes your men. Imagine what just one man can destroy with an arsenal and followers. I have set him up with an arms dealer who is working with us; he helps us, he becomes very rich; he's familiar with several high tech weapons and will deliver the goods tomorrow at noon … he will also have his own men with him. And stating the obvious, Colonel Blake has anticipated your arrival as well as your demise. These are the coordinates as of two hours ago. Good luck."

"According to SAT, Le Mur is calling from several places around the world simultaneously," the General said. I'm sending a team to assist your men to bring Colonel Blake back for trial; this hopefully will pan out."

"Sir, give us two days … an arms deal set up by one of the world's foremost terrorists, Le Mur, with his front man brokering the deal to lure Colonel Blake into a trap might work."

"Two days," the General was reluctant to agree.

David and six of his team flew to the island. Before they arrived at the coordinates, given by Le Mur, Colonel Blake called him.

"They're all dead, I have the weapons and I'm not returning home. I knew somehow you were involved in this, tracking me and that arms dealer, not too bright. Let's end this … he made you a Colonel; ludicrous. Let's see how well you fight. Your men are fools."

"And obviously, neither of us is coming alone for the showdown. You've waited a long time to bury me as you did the others who witnessed the massacre … and the faces of the villagers."

"I believed you could be loyal to me, follow my orders to Hell and back, but your loyalty was to Costanza and followed him. I'll call you with the new coordinates … meet in two hours."

They made the rendezvous at a small abandoned airport. Le Mur knew exactly where they were and followed.

"You sabotaged us at every turn, that's the death penalty. If the parcel had been intercepted by you … who knows."

Just then Blake delivered a blow to his chest, he was a third degree black belt. David retaliated with a kick to his face, Blake fell as he reached for his knife, somewhat surprised by David's martial arts fighting skills. David had told his men not to let Blake escape even if he defeated him. Blake ordered his men to do the same.

"You've been practicing," he said … "I violated Ana and would have told you to your face as you laid there dying … I would have killed the General if the MP hadn't shown up. I hated you so much, you just won't die."

The fighting intensified, the two had slugged one another for several minutes; the knives, the weapons of choice, had injured both.

"Colonel Mihn was to have tortured you and your men then kill everyone, even the two UN inspectors." The confessions came out.

"Did you think by killing me and seeing my face no more, you wouldn't see the faces of those you murdered, the senseless taking of innocent lives. I see their faces every night … so much hate and jealousy."

David was knocked down, he rolled to the side grabbed a large rock, throwing it, hitting Blake in the head; he was dazed for a few moments and dropped his knife.

"He always favored you, treated me like a second-class citizen; he's next on the list … you fight dirty like me, always challenging my authority."

"Can't let you do that." They fought over the knife.

"You got the girl, I'll deal with her, it won't be C-4 this time around. I am a Colonel … I deserve …"

"You deserve nothing." David was furious, they wrestled, beating one another physically challenging the other's strength as they were on the ground and fighting for control of the knife. "I take no pleasure in killing you but you can't be allowed to live after what you've done."

"And you think you can stop me?" Blake was now on top of David holding the knife to his throat. "Tell me first before I kill you … I sense your strength is going, who is Adrian Rodgers?"

David lost his focus for a moment, "Just what you see; nothing but an extraterrestrial astrophysicist with knowledge beyond our understanding." He could feel himself losing strength and control of the knife; he wondered if Adrian was there watching; he was.

"Then what came out of the ocean?" Blake wanted answers.

"His spaceship."

Just then with a last burst of energy, David turned the knife upward mortally wounding him, Colonel Blake hadn't expected to lose. "Now you can't bring me back. I'm glad it's over for one of us; no court martial … I hope you add my face to your dreams."

David stood up, "It didn't have to go this way, but as for dreams, now I can push the delete button and move on … it's over," David shouted to all who were listening, "go home."

"Kill that one, he's about to fire on Colonel Eisen." Suddenly there was a shot from several hundred feet away killing one of Blake's. Another shot was fired hitting another. Blake's men quickly dispersed fleeing the scene not taking the weapons.

Le Mur and those with him left. He called David. "The weapons are yours, you fought well … don't pursue me; have a good life."

David didn't have a chance to reply but he knew he would have to let General Gonzales and Le Mur settle their differences without interference.

"Colonel, who was helping us?" Ivan asked, "Preacher John didn't fire those shots."

"God only knows," David replied, but he knew.

"You fought good," Oaloff said. Away from everyone for the moment he then asked, "Was your Alien friend helping us?"

"I sense he was here ready to step in if needed." David smiled.

Blake's body and weapons were flown home; the Team paid for the funeral.

The General later spoke with David. "So what happened?"

"Blake saw through the arms deal, not realizing that Le Mur was behind the sale; he kills the dealer takes the weapons then changes the coordinates of our meeting to another location … we meet and basically winner takes all. He states his intention of using those weapons to further his plans to terrorize and massacre anyone standing in his way including us, so it didn't matter who won, his plans didn't include losing if he had to kill all of us. Two kill shots a few hundred feet away convinced Blake's army to disperse … Le Mur saved the day … we'll never find him. Blake died a bitter, miserable man; no one claimed the body so we had him buried, each man contributed." David was exhibiting relief and regret. "The weapons are secure."

"Any more details?"

"Sir, at this moment, I don't believe there are any I can think of."

"Then consider this case closed ... the Mogadishu incident was the sole decision of Colonel Blake and therefore bears the responsibility alone ... have your hand looked after. You and your men did well."

He and Ana announced their wedding date.

Adrian spoke with him about Earth's future. "We will be closely monitored by the Vegan Council as you know. The evolution process will take as long as it takes; humans, as you've pointed out, don't all think the same or have the same values. We will still be implementing steps to bring certain humans into the Think Tank. Discussions will include ways of growing foods, grain and animal sources, space exploration, medicines, the environment, new fuels, education on a broader scale, ways of stopping wars, diplomacy ... all are priority topics."

"That should keep us busy," David said, "war and terrorism, the connection to be addressed ... another thing comes to mind ... Ana is unable to bear children, we can adopt. I love her whatever; many women are childless."

Adrian said, "Then this could also be a priority topic."

~David's Journal~

2013 – 2017

Two years passed:

Several incidents had occurred that changed the world. Those who had committed to work together, from several countries, to defeat terrorism had refocused against each other over territorial acquisitions or crossing no-fly borders; with Turkey, a member of NATO, having shot down a Russian warplane crossing over its territory or Russia's intent to create an incident purposely to have a reason to move missiles into Syria, pointed toward Turkey, realizing that the Turks had a ninety kilometer open border where Nibus fighters could cross into Turkey and sell oil to them which essentially compromised the defeat of Nibus causing Vladimir Putin to say, "A stab in the back," refusing to back down from new sanctions initiated against the Turkish and President Recep Tayyip Erdogan who became president in 2014.

Turkey had allowed, in 2015, an American military presence at their Incirlik Air Base in order to shorten the distance on bombing runs against Nibus.

An attempted coup disrupting the government authority was quickly put down leaving President Erdogan in power; this was in 2016.

Fallujah in Iraq was the first city captured by Nibus and was freed two years later by coalition forces in 2016 dealing a devastating blow to the terrorist's forces. Many died.

Al-Raqqa, the epicenter of the Nibus held territory, taken in 2014 was liberated from Bashar al-Asad's regime forces even as Nibus made futile efforts to hold onto it.

The ongoing fight continued through 2016 to push Nibus out of Iraq and retake the city of Mosul, dealing a devastating loss to the enemy, as the Iraqi army joined forces with Kurdish Peshmerga forces, the military forces of the Autonomous region of Iraqi Kurdistan. Peshmerga is translated as 'one who confronts death'. The President of Iraqi Kurdistan is their formal head. Air support from part of the coalition has continued. Turkish troops are still supporting Peshmerga in the battle with artillery, tanks and tactical vehicles.

Syrians had begun to resettle certain areas of their homeland as others couldn't endure Nibus and their President-Dictator Bashar al-Asad who had killed millions in uprisings, having endured poverty and massacre; there were eleven million that were displaced. Bashar was still in power. The Syrian refugees were now in Europe and made their way to America. The vetting process was overloaded; terrorists would embed themselves in the many refugees; they would purposely not have papers which cleared them to enter several countries. No background checks then could be complete.

Terrorist groups promised a lie as they recruited young men and women possibly wanting husbands and adventure. For the first time, women who had joined, were being radicalized first then convincing husbands to become radicalized as well, willing to take the lives of soft targets ... murder for any reason. America had and continued to experience the result of that influence.

Beyond kidnappings and beheadings, mass murder of school children, came the call to murder CEO's of companies to destabilize the economies of nations around the world; it was having an effect.

Global warming was discussed at a conference in France where one hundred and ninety leaders of countries from around the world met. Fossil fuels were discussed at length; this was in 2015. The climate was improving just two years later.

Funding for terrorist activities in part came from looting more museums. Syria and Iraq were chief targets for thefts. Usually when the looting was complete, the largest of the artifacts, tall stone and quartz figures of ancient warriors, gods, famous statesmen and rulers were defaced then the museums were destroyed; destruction to satisfy thugs bent on erasing the past so they could create another.

An added note, the B-52s Statofortress, long range flying planes in 2016 made a comeback in the war against terror; the size of these 62-year-old bombers used in the Vietnam era were enormous as was their payload. They were retrofitted for modern warfare flying missions in the Gulf War by dedicated individuals and piloted by dedicated crews and now to be flown again in the latest war in the Middle East.

There was a meeting with the General and members of his Team. Representatives from the State Department, two men David knew, Museum Curator Dr. Maleke, Vicki Amimour his assistant and Dr. Cook, director of Ancient Relics Recoveries in the Middle East.

"Colonel Eisen," the General began, "you are aware of the looting and destruction of several museums in Syria and Iraq. Dr. Maleke and his assistant Ms. Amimour are curators at the Education Heritage Museum in Aleppo Province."

Dr. Maleke then spoke. "Our museum has been attacked, looting here occurred, but not destroyed. We have lost several priceless relics but it's as if there is something there they're waiting for."

"Are you certain its Nibus?" David asked Dr. Cook.

"Not totally, but usually this is their way. Jams Ratcliff knows about these things; he returns property, lost or stolen if he can find who the property belongs to as Director of Recoveries at the Art Loss Register in England. He is quoted, 'People are digging up things that haven't been seen for thousands of years ... but unlike stolen art, no one knows what it is or who to return it to.' That's where I come in ... I have studied archelogy dating back thousands of years and usually can identify regions that the artifacts came from."

Dr. Maleke said, "Islamic State militants began destroying cultural heritage sites soon after the group seized large areas of Iraq and Syria; but Syrian Archaeologist Amr al-Azm said, 'Looting is not always specific to territory controlled by the Islamic State'; but I believe it's Nibus," he said.

"We have heard of a secret chamber built below the museum floor containing the most treasured of the artifacts ... and not all of the artifacts were destroyed," Dr. Cook replied. "We will return these at some point to the museum if there is one left or somewhere else."

"So this destruction will spread throughout the Middle East if not stopped and Dr. Maleke is urging our help now," the General said.

"Boots on the ground can't protect all of the museums and are there other museums that are rumored to have secret chambers?" David asked.

"Not to our knowledge," Vicki replied.

"I ask only for help with this one," Dr. Maleke pleaded. "Rescue what's left, find the hidden chamber if there is one."

"Major Oaloff is occupied with half the Team in Arabia and suggests you take command of this mission Colonel," the General said.

David hesitates for a moment then, "Tell Major Oaloff I accept." Three of his men were there and agreed.

"Nibus will be watching ... they have most certainly heard the rumor."

The men who would be in on the mission knew the dangers.

"A small Syrian force is there to help, around fifteen, keeping the enemy at bay. Depart for Aleppo Province tomorrow. Two cranes and other machinery will be aboard as well as armament. Rescue those at the museum and the relics that can be saved to be delivered to Menagh Airbase in Aleppo; if you encounter enemy fire, you have permission from the Turkish government to cross the border to Incirlik Airbase. The Russians will be doing flyhys to dissuade Nibus troops in the area."

"We'll need two Chinooks; the larger objects can be carried in two sling loads each if it comes to it, and two pilots to fly the second ship."

"Already anticipated ... leave tomorrow 0800 hours."

They arrived on the museum grounds; they met to discuss coordination of the fifteen Syrian troops as well as the museum curator and staff.

"As you can see, so many things were taken," one told them.

"We have to work quickly," David said, "inventories, what goes and that chamber."

They did. Vicki Amimour was the highest ranking one there after the Curator Dr. Maleke; there were ten staff. The equipment was moved into the museum, everyone was given a brief tour checking for explosives and all exits.

Vicki and Dr. Maleke then showed three areas where the chamber might be located containing the most prized of all the relics. A thermal imaging device was then used before beginning to penetrate the marble floors where the secret compartment was.

"It's there", Pettigrew said, "we can't detonate, we'll destroy everything. Don't know the structural integrity."

"Vinnie, Sunrise, do your thing," David ordered.

They used a laser cutting tool requiring two to hold it. Private Kline, who came with them and two Syrian soldiers removed pieces of the floor as it was cut. Several hours later they reached an area where there were stairs; they donned masks as protection from dust and particles.

"The stairs seem intact." Two soldiers accompanied Dr. Maleke, Vicki and David downstairs.

"We need lights and the generators." Four sets of high voltage generators and lights were set up.

Parts of the floor became unstable and had to be removed.

Everyone was taking shifts as well as the Syrians, who were keeping an eye out for terrorist movements and had agreed to help moving and loading the artifacts; guarding, moving or loading were the most important, then near exhaustion came sleep.

David gave encrypted updates indicating progress. Gun shots were heard. "More to keep us alert that Nibus is watching," he told the General.

The small observation drones were pinpointing enemy locations using infrared cameras at night. They used a signaling beacon to alert air or ground forces in the area to their presence at the museum not to strike. Nibus, however, was closing in on their prize. Schwartz and Preacher John kept firing in the direction of the terrorists from the roof as was necessary. Stingers were used by the Syrians as well as automatic weapons, wounding the enemy.

"They won't be firing stingers or mortars at the museum which would destroy any artifacts; the Chinooks will provide transportation for the artifacts if they kill us, or be destroyed if they cannot stop us any other way," Vinnie said as Dr. Maleke and Sunrise listened.

Hours went by. "We need more time General, everyone is pitching in, even the Syrians are taking shifts; the hidden chamber, having been sealed for over a hundred years, has taken much of our time. There are artifacts beyond belief … several treasures have been crated and loaded … but not the 'scroll', if it even exists."

"Don't become casualties; you have a 24-hour extension, scroll or no scroll."

"Yes Sir."

"And David, there might be a Nibus sympathizer in your midst. Someone, feminine is making repeated calls from the museum on a satellite phone to a suspected dealer in the Turkish city of Ankara who is connected to a collector of rare art and antiquities in the U.S."

"Copy that Sir".

Vicki had made several phone calls in the time since David and his men arrived; she had just made another, always private.

"Who were you calling?" David asked her.

"Who were you talking to?" she retorted.

"My boss," he said. "Everything is ok … he's given us an additional 24-hour extension."

"Wonderful … I was talking to family, I didn't tell them about what is going on here with the museum."

They share a meal as they rest. "What are your plans when this is over?"

"I'll try for another museum hopefully in a safer area, go on excavations perhaps with Dr. Maleke. I respect him, as I do archaeologist Amr al-Azm; you saw him on the internet." Just then her phone rang again, she left. "I'll be right back." Five entered the room to rest. David, suspicious from the beginning wouldn't question her further.

As she returned, two fragmentation grenades crashed through a window, "Shrapnel," David shouted, then another which he grabbed and threw back in a cook off; he quickly covered her as he held her close. He and others were cut as more grenades were thrown. Gunfire was heard as Preacher John and Schwartz fired on their attackers wounding four and killing one.

"Everyone ok?" Dr. Maleke yelled.

"We've all been hit," David said.

"Not me." Vicki was ok.

"Medic?"

"I'm hit but nothing serious."

None had life threatening injuries.

"Thank you for saving me." Vicki didn't express her emotions very often when it came to meeting someone. "You married?"

He was startled by the question. "Happily … kids."

"All the good ones are taken," she said and smiled; they began to work quickly even while wounded.

Each artifact was photographed and tagged; several had been moved into heavy crates protected by thick padding.

Later, another call. David eavesdropped, he had a translator attached to his phone. She returned.

"You making a deal with the enemy?"

"I am not a terrorist."

"Really."

"I am an archaeologist working with the police about to broker a deal with a Turkish dealer in Ankara who will take these antiquities and sell them to an American businessman. Get the scrolls at any cost I was told … we don't know who he is; we suspect."

"So how will you proceed – does anyone else know?"

"Not outside the police. We'll catch the businessman by greed … a big payday for Nibus, they believe."

"How come you're involved in something so dangerous?"

"I was tempted once, and now I am paying back for my crime."

"Vicki, Colonel," someone yelled, come quickly, "we have found it, the scroll."

"The one," Vinnie said.

"Thousands of years old, written by Plato himself."

"We were about to give up," Dr. Cook said, "I must call Jams Ratcliff and Amr al-Azm."

"Here, right under our noses," Dr. Maleke said. Everyone stopped for a few moments to view the manuscript; it was inside an airtight, glass container. He examined it without removing it. "It must be opened in an air free environment to be studied; in air it would disintegrate immediately. Whoever placed it here many years ago knew this. It's more valuable than anything here ... we must get back to work."

"We have less than 24-hours," Pettigrew reminded them.

The two Chinooks were loaded. Sunrise and another pilot carefully calculated the weight and balance of both. The two cranes would be left to the Syrians; they had their own transport. As many artifacts as possible were taken. Two crates each in slingload, were tethered to the underside of each Chinook when the last of the smaller relics were inside.

"We're on our way," he told the General. "The Syrian help is leaving after we do ... I expressed our thanks."

"Everyone on board," Sunrise said. It was almost dawn; there were weapons aboard to defend the aircraft.

They reached the Menagh Airbase but were fired on by Nibus.

"Go for the Turkish border," David ordered as they returned fire ... "Incirlik Airbase."

They made it. Arrests were made for the Turkish dealer who gave up the information naming the buyer, an American; their arrests came swiftly as their monetary abilities had allowed for a sale of ancient artifacts for a large profit to Nibus. They later destroyed the museum. Their accounts were frozen and seized as both and possibly others associated with the deal would face prison time aiding the enemy. David related the events to the General.

Some months later the coveted scroll was studied and put on display at another museum along with other artifacts.

David and Ana traveled with Adrian to the area of the Dead Sea to visit other historical sites and participate in unearthing precious relics with others interested in visiting the past; two museums were visited.

CHAPTER TWO

~David's Journal~

Five years passed:

Wars had been averted in several areas of the world through diplomacy while others were waged as the human condition festered like a sore due to disease and poverty; deteriorating conditions resulting from various events initiated by their respective dictators and terrorist groups which held their countries hostage; Nibus and Al Qaeda, two of the largest terrorist groups, took advantage of these conditions promising a lie of making life better as they recruited other factions to join. They had used the internet to recruit followers, who had no previous affiliation with any terrorist group, who longed to belong; usually young people lured by a sense of adventure, even the privileged were joining. The soft targets, as always, were the most vulnerable; many were encouraged to arm themselves wherever they went. There were many 'lone wolves' going it alone, ready to kill for whatever the cause of the day was; terrorism never stopped whatever form it took.

Mass genocide was discussed with certain world leaders and its role in suppressing those who fought for freedom. Witnesses pointed out areas where citizens and family members were buried in mass graves; torture was rampant. Many were injured as chlorine, mustard and sarin gas were used, as well as barrel bombs, on dissidents, rebels determined to change things, secretly filmed and given to the free press; several had testified to these events. Mutilations were rampant of Christians, Jews and dissidents.

David continued to teach and TA for Adrian, as time permitted, before being put on active duty again; he remained as mission specialist assisting in planning each mission for Orion's Belt. Several leaders in the Middle East were familiar with him as he had traveled with American Diplomat Robert Selby on occasion to meet with them where American troops were fighting beside the armies of those countries against terrorism. He and Adrian both lectured young college students to be all they could be without doing harm to others and joining the Think Tank as a better alternative promoting a future, a future of equality and peace.

Ana was a member of All Saints Catholic Church. David wasn't a religious man but did believe in something greater and attended with her. He couldn't yet reconcile that God, if he existed, would allow war and famine. They had triplets, now four-years-old. He could see a miracle when he looked at them; he loved his family. From Ana's first scream, "I think I'm pregnant, I feel strange … I can't be pregnant … that's impossible;" then after a visit to the gynecologist, who couldn't believe it either, "David, I'm pregnant."

"That's not possible," he said.

Months later she delivered. David suspected Adrian was somehow involved; he was considered a member of the family and was totally fascinated with human birth, especially this birth. He doted on the two girls and one boy. They had a propensity to study astrophysics and view the stars, even as small children.

As a family, they would have to deal with the reality of the times, protecting themselves and the children. Ana now carried a pistol that David gave her; she became proficient as she learned how to use it. A plain clothes security agent, provided by the Army, was assigned to accompany her everywhere and the children. David, as always took a weapon everywhere, every day, but he refused to have his own security agent. "Another CEO was murdered; ten so far, HNN reported."

"Where to now?" Adrian was concerned about a peace keeping mission.

"To North Korea … I'm not looking forward to it as this mission is to gain release of four Americans being held hostage as spies. The dictator had his father murdered; the son, Chul-Moo, assumed the position of Supreme Leader. His name means 'weapon of iron', he hates Americans and has a reputation of brutality as he imprisoned several political activists. I'll be traveling with Diplomat Selby. One of the prisoners is working for us, a spy, a Korean who has American citizenship and defected to work on weapons development in Korea … monitoring their progress on developing more ballistic missiles, more destructive than ever before. Korea is demonstrating its destructive power to intimidate the world into giving them what they want, a trade agreement and to remove the boundaries of the DMZ separating North and South."

"Does Ana know the danger involved on this one?"

"No, I promised her I was out of the …"

Just then Ana walked in. "Are you discussing that vacation to Italy you promised?"

"Yes, and I'll get the heads up from the General as to when." He looked at Adrian then, "Cecily and Grant will take care of the kids at Ana's while we're gone. Adrian, you'll have the run of the house at my place … or stay here with them … probably two weeks."

Ana agreed and left them alone to talk.

"You're apprehensive … continue what you were telling me."

"Korea is under lockdown, we can't arouse suspicion there that one spy will tip the balance in America's decision to deny any agreement. All of us could be captured or killed; as far as help, it would appear we have no one on the inside who would help. The Dictator doesn't trust anyone and recently executed two top aides along with other military advisors for disagreeing with him. My men would be captured or executed the minute they set foot in the country … technically they are under Lieutenant Colonel Oaloff's command."

Later, "It might be a week," he told Ana, "that I'll be gone."

"What are you not telling me?"

"I can't discuss this …"

"Top secret? Dangerous?"

David hesitated … "Yes. It involves having our national security measures hacked." He didn't tell her about the mission to rescue the four hostages, one of which was a scientist pretending to have defected to Korea renouncing his American Citizenship.

Days passed, "Will you be here when I return?" He wouldn't risk losing her.

"Honestly, I'm so angry ... I gave you my heart and now you're breaking it."

"You won't let me touch you."

She tried not to be angry even as tears flowed. "And what do I tell the children if you don't return? You're not telling me everything."

He held her. "If it meant making a better world for us and our children, would it be worth it?"

"Don't ask me that because I can't answer ... make love to me."

They did.

He was at the Base the next morning going over final instructions with the General, Oaloff and Diplomat Selby whether to postpone or proceed. There were six unfamiliar faces attending the meeting – representatives from six nations surrounding Korea. A scientist is in on the meeting, a bomb expert and physicist, Dr. O'Keefe who put his spin on the news that came from a Korean scientist, a spy, working in Korea.

"At first, I couldn't, wouldn't believe it, not yet, I kept telling myself, but detecting equipment flown into the sky has detected particles to authenticate the threat from Korea as a reality. Korea has a superior hydrogen bomb. They have tested the smaller version. Atomic bombs use nuclear fission, splitting the atom. Korea has had atomic bomb capabilities for years. Hydrogen bombs use nuclear fusion, like the activity in our sun – a thermonuclear reaction. Put simply, the division of one atom into two is atomic fission; fusion is the combination of two lighter atoms into a larger one, used in nuclear power reactors. Uranium 235 is produced in accelerators breaking into smaller particles merging elements into a whole. We must anticipate the acts of a crazy man and stop him if possible."

"What would you suggest?" one asked.

The meeting went on for an hour as suggestions were made.

Ana was seeing her next patient at the office; she was distracted and nervous. "Cancel the rest of the day," Ana told her secretary, "I'm feeling sick;" this was unusual for Ana. It was late afternoon, the agent was with her as she shopped for groceries. Suddenly he was gone – no answer on his cell phone, then two men on either side of her walked across the street.

"Don't yell or scream, come with us; the agent will live."

There was no way she could defend herself even with the pistol she carried everywhere.

"Call him," another told her.

She did. "Don't look for me, I'm being taken somewhere out of the country by private jet, the agent is at the store unharmed."

One of the kidnappers took the phone, "Keep your appointment with the Supreme Leader in two days, push for the trade agreement, then we'll talk."

"Don't harm her;" the call was terminated. The General and Diplomat were notified.

"The Korean Dictator is desperate at this point and likely to do anything to get what he wants." Two others from the government met with them. "Normally I would say don't go but he has a bargaining chip, Colonel Eisen's wife," the General spoke somberly.

The next day they were on a private jet accompanied by two security agents to Korea. A Korean security detail met them hours later. From the airport they were escorted to the presidential palace. They were welcomed, wined and dined; the young Supreme Leader Chul-Moo, who followed in his father's footsteps, was lukewarm and calloused to his guests. David restrained himself in not asking about Ana.

Afterward, Diplomat Selby began, "We want to bring home the four hostages, one of which has been working for you as a scientist, forsaking America and revealing our progress in the nuclear, hydrogen bomb business; and perhaps there is now a fifth hostage, Ana Eisen, wife of the Colonel, kidnapped two days ago."

Chul-Moo became hostile, "So you're asking for them but not discussing a trade agreement or removal of the DMZ boundary which we have asked for. We are defined as terrorists against our own people."

"Defined as intolerant of free speech," Diplomat Selby replied. "Mass killings of even your generals who disagree with you, threats of annihilation for the whole world threatening us all with your hydrogen bombs; are these acts of terrorists? You further isolate yourselves from any help."

"The South and the U.S. have the Free Trade Agreement, we can begin there," Chul-Moo kept the pressure on, "and we give you Ana Eisen."

"The Republic of South Korea and the U.S. are deepening our strong bilateral economic trade and investment relations, lowering trade barriers, benefiting both countries since the treaty was first signed, as you know, on June 30, 2007 and a renegotiation signed in 2010. Free trade always encourages economic growth and creates more jobs," Diplomat Selby said. "Seoul also wanted products made by South Korean companies in the Kaesong Industrial Region in North Korea in the deal; Washington did not. The disagreement will be unresolved for the time being."

The General and his Lieutenant stood up as the bodyguards that arrived with Diplomat Selby and David were taken to confined quarters as they protested.

"They will not be harmed as you both will be my guests for the evening, not captives, not prisoners. See what trouble you are in ... coming here expecting me to do your bidding ... What do I get in return?"

"I'm sure Colonel Eisen would like to see his wife."

The Supreme Leader was playing his hand having everyone concerned at his mercy. "Guards, take the guests to the facility;" he looked confident, then, "I will join you later, then you may question the scientist and someone who is anxious to see you Colonel."

David quickly goes accompanied by two guards; a doctor is suturing a wound on her leg.

"Almost finished, she fell ... my regrets; have it checked once you reach home ... shouldn't have happened," he said nervously.

Unknown to anyone, the doctor and scientist had earlier collaborated to put a chip inside her leg revealing hours of data on the nuclear progress and capabilities of Korea and their long range goals of threating surrounding countries beginning with South Korea and eventually attacking the U.S.

David held her; she hadn't been tortured. He questioned her, she recognized him but said very little. She had been drugged and remained tied to a chair.

"She was questioned," the Doctor said. "Less stressful and the wound."

"Release her ... now."

"I cannot do that ... orders. I will check on her later; the guard will watch out for her."

He kissed her. "Where are the other hostages?'

He was taken to another area. They were accused of being spies. They told their stories of being innocent. "They want to kill us ... tourists." They were in reality tourists who had another agenda, that of smuggling out the chip now implanted in Ana's leg; they were searched but no chip was found. They didn't know where the chip was.

"Diplomat Selby is working on your release as well as my wife Ana; we're doing our best," David told them.

"Please get us out of here ... before they harm us."

David looked at them but said nothing more.

Afterward, David and Diplomat Selby visited with the scientist along with the Dictator and his highest ranking general. He had been tortured but didn't admit to being an American spy upon being questioned.

"We have no agenda here except to grow as a country, in peace," he said.

Diplomat Selby countered, "Then why threaten the world with nuclear annihilation? Is that hydrogen bomb a myth, more powerful, more deadly?"

The question wasn't answered as they talked for several minutes. David and the Diplomat were then escorted to other areas of the City away from the nuclear power plant demonstrating businesses, beauty and growth.

"Release her," David said.

"Not so fast." Chul-Moo had a plan to pressure David and Diplomat Selby into compliance, doing his bidding. Both were later escorted to separate rooms for the night with guards posted everywhere down the long hallway.

David was brought to him for a private conversation early the next morning.

"I have a deal for you ... in exchange, you and your wife will be freed. Kill my top General as well as his lieutenant who disagrees with me continually on how Korea should be run, as he plans staging a coup against me soon to seize power; he has the military backing him ... also you must kill Diplomat Selby."

"So that's why she was kidnapped, to pressure me to create an international incident to win support for this trade agreement and removal of the DMZ boundary. You realize I'll be tried for murder; there's no real escape."

"But you will live, she will live ... you'll be flown anywhere in the world. A black eye for America, that a Colonel, a diplomat of sorts, will turn the tide for us. I am taking Korea into a new era, a new direction; domination of this part of the world by fear and in time the shadow of Korea will cover the world ... she will be brought to you this evening; discuss the matter."

"The hostages?"

"They will remain with us."

Ana was allowed an hour to be with David; she fell asleep in his arms. He voiced his concerns to Adrian. "I hope you're here somewhere."

"I have heard everything. Every time I interfere, it puts your world at risk; those on the Council want the Earth to be spared but allowing humans to do the negotiating, to do what's necessary with minimal help from me. But I cannot stand by and see courageous people die for nothing when they are keeping the world safe for another day."

"I won't cooperate with them."

"I know ... I will do something."

Adrian then appeared in the General's bedroom that evening; he lived a few miles from the palace. He was frightened and pointed a gun at Adrian. "Who or what are you?"

"Your weapon will have no effect on me ... your murder has been planned for tomorrow as the Supreme Leader is having a meeting to discuss a trade agreement; he plans to have Colonel Eisen assassinate you and your lieutenant before you can stage a coup at tomorrow's meeting ... he wants to control the military, also to kill Diplomat Selby and the scientist, creating an international incident and gain America's help in pressuring other nations to vote for a trade agreement. He plans to take Korea in a new direction, one of terror. If you want to live, do as I suggest. Prepare tonight, don't harm Colonel Eisen who will pretend to obey the Supreme Leader; when it's over, take the Colonel, his wife, Diplomat Shelby and the hostages including the scientist, to a jet and have them flown to America."

The General agreed to everything. "Who or what are you?"

Adrian briefly changed form, then back, "Call me a guardian of this planet. The Supreme Leader knows nothing about me, nor does the world for that matter; let's keep it that way."

The next day, seven people sat around a large table to discuss the possibility of getting the agreement. The Supreme Leader looked over at David who now stood up. He produced a gun which had been taped under his chair.

"I believe this is your gun," he said as he walked over to him holding the gun in a non-threatening manner and lays it on the table. "I cannot do as you ask, even if my wife, who you have imprisoned here, and I are executed; my orders from you to assassinate the General, his lieutenant and Diplomat Selby, giving you control of the military, won't be from my hand."

Everyone in the room was silent for a few moments; the Supreme Leader stood up and would have killed David himself, but the General pointed a gun at him and called in more soldiers.

"You could have told me David," Diplomat Selby said.

"No Sir, I couldn't."

"Get going," the General shouted. "Follow the guards to the jet; your wife is waiting." David motioned a thank you. Ana was now aware she carried the valuable chip.

The Supreme Leader ordered the jet to be shot down suspecting those aboard carried valuable information. The General belayed the order and threatened him with an accidental early death if he attempted to have the General assassinated again.

Ana was traumatized, David held her. Diplomat Selby, his two security and three of the American hostages were allowed to leave; the young scientist wasn't. Adrian had read his mind and knew about the devastation the Supreme Leader had planned in the way of weapons research and use. All would be debriefed upon arriving in America; there would be no trade agreement anytime soon and the boundaries of the DMZ remained.

They revealed what the scientist had told them; the centrifuges were up and running, more weapons grade uranium, more missiles and a possible coup led by the Supreme Leader's top General.

"Who's in charge?" The General and three from a government committee asked.

The Korean general would always remember meeting Adrian and wondered what he could have done in the way of retaliation on behalf of those he protected; nevertheless, Korea would pursue domination through intimidation.

New wars caused David to be placed on active status again. He and Ana had come to an understanding as the world was changing. Italy would wait. Terrorists from within had brought the wars closer to home. The Think Tank reached out to those who might be recruited by Nibus and to those 'lone wolves' looking for any cause to wreak destruction in some form. It was essentially a cyber war to prevent the enemy from hacking into sensitive areas as banks, defense and hundreds of other American agencies and now the Pentagon which had been hacked in 2015.

The cyber abilities of some were extraordinary, being able to shut down missile defense systems across the ocean and cause fluctuations in enemy communication. One new tactic that showed promise required a group of male hackers to reach out to possible female recruits being radicalized by Nibus, but appearing shirtless while on line and encouraging them to not seek mates overseas and kill for them; "Stay here, marry one of us and you won't have to kill anybody." It was having a positive effect.

David was sent to Iraq as an observer and advisor helping in matters of strategy on the battlefield and to bring a cohesion between the Iraqi and American troops fighting together to take back Anbar Province from the terrorists. Iraq had sought the help to stop Nibus even as they had abandoned a strategically important base in Anbar Province; this occurred in 2013. As fighting had continued in the area, Al Qaeda had been another terrorist faction growing rapidly as it competed with Nibus who had displaced several million in Syria. Nigeria's Boko Haram terrorists were strengthening ties with the Islamic State Group; murder in Anbar. Adrian knew all of this as David and he conferred for progress reports to the Vegan Council. Fighting over the same territories would continue for years.

The Iraqi forces were outnumbered and outgunned as they fought both insurgents and terrorists. Newer American armament and tactical armored vehicles were given to even the odds as was the training. Fighting for certain areas, as Anbar, was crucial to stopping the Sunni led Nibus who spilled over the border of Iraq daily from Iran, the largest state sponsor of terror. David and two others, military, arrived.

"To those of you who don't know him, this is Colonel Eisen. I received training under his command as did several of you ... he is a strategist and analyst, here to observe and will, if needed, confer with me on any changes to defeat the enemy; I respect him," Lieutenant Colonel Oaloff said. Then saluted him, they shook hands.

"I appreciate that Colonel, you and your men have my respect; as he stated, we'll be working together changing strategy if necessary as we face Nibus head on, holding our position here."

There were two hundred American forces stationed at Base camp thirty-miles from the battle zone where barracks and tents dotted the area along with a first rate medical facility. Helicopters as well as tactical armored vehicles, as Humvees, were on Base; drones for observation and drones carrying missiles could be launched at a moments notice. Cyber units were stationed there communicating with those at the battlefront who also had the same communication abilities and arsenal as well as observation drones. Colonel Oaloff had reminded everyone that the CPT, cyber units, would affect the outcome of the war as if standing by those in combat, holding a weapon.

The terrorists initiated their assault first, focused on reaching the American-Iraqi Base camp, first having to pass through the allied line of defense, the remains of a small town damaged by mortar fire now occupied by the allies. David was stationed in one of the buildings with one CPT and two soldiers. Thirty men drew a line in the sand that day.

The weapons fire grew louder, mortars from both sides. Oaloff could be heard, "Weapons hot – light `em up;" the saw machine guns fired 120 RMP.

Another yelled, "They're coming with reinforcements ... circling around us." AK-47s were largely used by the enemy as they barricaded themselves behind rubble partly buried in the sand; it was noon there, the heat was unrelenting; the coalition forces retaliated with the AR-15s, British 717s and M-4 Carbines with 203 grenade launchers attached. Stinger missiles were fired at the buildings as well as at any drones or any air support flying above as the enemy moved over a hill to take control. David had left his observation post to lend his support firing his Glock pistol wounding one, killing another who tried to shut down the communication between the allies and Base camp. A knife fight ensued as one of the terrorists fired his weapon wounding him.

"Sir," one of the two guards found him.

"Only a flesh wound," he said. "This one will live to be interrogated."

The Allies were hit with fragmentation grenades, the most devastating kind due to shards of metal shooting in all directions; they retaliated with several 'cook offs'. Several on both sides had sustained injuries; two medical personnel addressed the injuries before evacuating the seriously injured to Base, but their route was now blocked by a tactical reinforced vehicle resembling a tank carrying several of the enemy, which now remained stationary. The enemy were sure of a victory as night fell. The communications were also disrupted.

"Sitting ducks Sir," one of Colonel Oaloff's said. "Our weapons have been compromised by an infiltrator."

"They're in the buildings," Oaloff said and a drone strike isn't possible without mass casualties to our side."

"We have to find the rat."

Satellite phones would alert the enemy as well but David's was the only encrypted one. Oaloff made the call.

The orders were to "Hold position, a drone will be sent to scan the area." The enemy shot it down using a stinger but not before a thermal image of the enemy within was taken. They found him after being alerted where he was, sabotaging the allied weapons in one of the buildings. Quickly he was apprehended; parts of the weaponry were recovered and reworked, everyone participated. Oaloff and David worked one of the shifts.

"Time to play rough?"

"Brought both," Oaloff said. "One Manpad, one RPG-7; these he didn't sabotage."

There was a meeting as to how they would proceed. Another tactical vehicle joined the first. The RPG-7 was prepared, dawn was approaching. The weapon was fired at one of the two enemy vehicles; it was blown beyond recognition. The second that had fired at the coalition was destroyed as well. The men cheered even as gunfire was heard as the battle continued. A helicopter flew overhead dropping a barrel bomb of mustard gas meant to blind and suffocate. The Manpad surface to air missile – air defense system was fired destroying the helicopter and all aboard but not before the barrel bomb found its target. Miraculously the injuries weren't severe. A haboob began to manifest itself prompting Oaloff to order a cease fire. Strong winds carried the thick sand two hundred feet high as it moved over the battle scene; the hot sand burned any exposed skin as they wrapped scarves around their faces or anything available and waited out the storm. "Cease fire," came the order.

Several minutes later the haboob had passed; the battle didn't resume as the enemy, over the hill, lay buried. They took the brunt of the storm having been hit the hardest.

Three days later, David and Oaloff said their goodbyes; they had worked together strategizing how to defeat the enemy with minimum casualties.

"Be safe," David said, "when you return, we'll celebrate; bring everyone from the group."

"Just expect us, we'll be there. And Ana? … second set of triplets?"

"Soon; we're considering birth control … seriously." David laughed.

"Any more missions with the Diplomat?"

"Not to Korea."

Adrian knew about the battle but denied maneuvering the weather sending the sandstorm to kill the enemy. David didn't believe him.

David prepared to come home after being involved in two separate conflicts around the world. On his way back to Base camp in Iraq, the General congratulated him giving high praise to all that had participated in the Iraqi-American coalition fighting Nibus. "Well done Colonel and to the Lieutenant Colonel."

David replied, "Thank you Sir ... there were those injured but not seriously and one infiltrator, Iraqi, who sabotaged us destroying part of our weaponry."

"This is putting a lot on you now, but I am giving you new orders. I need you and whoever you choose to take on a mission today to Kabul, Afghanistan for an extraction. Hotak, our friend, who has given us good intel on the Taliban situation there, has been arrested and will most likely be tortured for what he has told us."

David was very adamant to see him rescued as well. "After we reach Base and rearm, we will be on our way ... I need only two with me."

"David, this might be an execution by our side if we can't extract him; if he is tortured, and they won't be quick, even if he told them everything ... no one should endure that."

"Understood Sir ... if a rescue is not possible."

"This will be difficult for all of us – a friend who has saved countless American lives ... at least we were able to save his family."

"Understood General."

"Be safe."

The next morning, having had minimal sleep, David and two others were on a forested hill, looking into the town square. The Taliban had already begun to torture him; he was brought out as an example to the other villagers and tied against a wall of metal bars. The Taliban didn't care how loved and respected this sixty-year-old husband and father of three was to the village. They had begun this interrogation the night before cutting and maiming him; his cries in pain were felt by David and the two with him ... hours passed. "No hope of rescue yet," he said, "too many innocent civilians – causalities will be too high," he told the General.

"Then you must terminate him and take out as many of the Taliban in the process."

David prepared himself to kill a friend; it was emotional. "Where are you Corporal?" He positioned his two men strategically to execute as many of the enemy as possible helping the villagers.

"A click away at your eight o'clock sir."

"Private?"

"Now at your three o'clock Commander."

"If we can't reach him then I terminate him; take out as many Taliban without killing the villagers."

The torture continued as he was repeatedly maimed. Hotak looked up toward David, not seeing him, but knowing that he was there, shouted the words, "Do it ... now." A single gunshot rang out killing him, the villagers ran for cover, the Taliban was no match. All were killed or critically injured. A quick escape was made over a hill and into a waiting Humvee, then headed for the helicopter that would bring them home; their emotions were mixed.

The General debriefed him, discouraging other missions. "Be with your wife and children ... continue with planning the missions."

Ana hoped he wouldn't travel overseas for a while, since the birth of a second set of triplets a week later, a record book occurrence in their respective families; both Ana and David then had procedures done for birth control and hired more help. Adrian had him teaching again and assisting him as TA.

David and Adrian had compiled reports over five years for the Vegan Council; both realized that time was running out for planet Earth. "This is what we must tell them," Adrian said:

{The Supreme Leader of Iran, Ayatollah Ali Khamenei, having constitutional authority over judiciary, regular armed forces and the Elite Revolutionary Guards had in 2015, pushed America and other nations for a nuclear deal that would effectively push back the development of nuclear weapons development for ten years in exchange for removing sanctions and paying billions to Iran for such a deal; the deal failed five years later; 'the great Satan', they called us and now have many missiles aimed at several countries including America. This happened under our current president.

Terrorists continue destroying history as they raid museums continually; they have turned terror on their own people as more Muslims are attacked. In 2015 they struck on Ramadan, their holy day, destroying a Tunisian Mosque and all inside; these attacks continue from Mosques to schools to marketplaces, anywhere, beheading those who teach peace. Many coalition troops have died fighting to stop the senseless killings which continue; wars end, wars begin, global turmoil. Children were being used to carry their explosives to certain areas, some as young as ten dying for a cause they didn't understand.

Russians and Kurds have banded together to save what is left of Syria and promising to protect those who want to return. American forces are stationed in certain areas as peacekeepers. Bashar al-Asad is still in power.

The free world has become more nervous as people are murdered for no reason. Nibus and Al Qaeda are the two major terror factions as of 2020. Everyone now in America carries a gun.}

Three months passed; the men he had commanded had a cookout and discussed the war in Fallujah as well as their next missions. David continued to advise and plan future ones under the command of Lieutenant Colonel Oaloff. David wouldn't be deployed for the time being if ever. Attacks were becoming frequent in the free world as terrorists became bolder keeping everyone on edge and vigilant.

Ana and David were very much in love and were proud to show off their youngest children, two boys and one girl. Italy could wait a while longer. Three months later they went; two security also accompanied them and enjoyed the trip. Several volunteered besides Adrian, Cecily and Grant to care for the now six children and provide security at the house. Adrian stayed at David's while Cecily and Grant and the children were at Ana's, since he could arrive in an instant, he made frequent visits.

Five miles away was a favorite computer store and repair shop. Both Ana and David had visited Griffin's Electronics on numerous occasions; it was owned and run by father and son.

A young blond woman, tall, around thirty, entered the store and met Kyle, the son; he was immediately attracted to her as she talked with him.

"I'm Mindy, this is my boyfriend's laptop – its hard drive has shut down."

"Crashed," he said, "I'm Kyle."

"Well Kyle, can you fix it and the password is Edward 55."

He couldn't believe how naïve she was giving the password; he checked the computer, "Probably next week … we're running behind."

"You're very smart to be doing this."

"I'm just geared to this, it's not that I'm very smart … what do you do?"

"I'm a model at Della's … you're really cute."

He blushed. "Well I'm putting three days and we'll call you if anything else is detected. Certainly don't tell him you gave me his password."

"He's been so odd lately, buying guns, night vison goggles and supplies."

"That doesn't seem odd … does he hunt?"

"He says he goes hunting, I never go, guns frighten me. Well, I better get home and cleanup the maps and other papers – he comes home in two days."

"Well, good luck."

She left, Kyle called his father … "I'm staying late to change out a hard drive; be there in an hour or so." He had taken the computer to put it on a shelf but decided instead to follow a hunch; something didn't feel right. He used the password and read the email; recruiting propaganda for becoming a terrorist. This alarmed him so he took a flash drive and saved all the information including correspondence. He then carefully put the computer on a shelf to be repaired, he called David.

"I need you to see this."

David arrived soon after, "Did you get it on a flash drive?"

"Yes, but I can't say I started repairs. According to her, he doesn't know she brought the computer here and gave me the password; he should be home from a road trip in just under two days."

"Don't fix anything."

"I won't; I don't know if she's married to the guy … they live together – she says he's been acting odd lately, fixating on weapons."

"Be careful Kyle ... if he even suspects."

"Got it."

Together they studied the information on the flash drive. David alerted the General. For the time being he would work with Kyle as an employee; he pretended to not be with the military but a disgruntled arms expert working on electronics.

Two days passed, Mindy and her friend Scott stopped by the electronics store.

"I don't want my computer fixed," he said nervously.

"And your name is ..."

"Scott."

"We haven't had a chance to look at it ... we're backlogged."

"That's good news; she brought in the wrong computer ... dizzy blond."

Kyle bristled hearing her called that as he got the computer and gave it to Scott. He had put a used hard drive, that did work, into the computer and downloaded all the information and contents into the newer hard drive hoping that Scott would continue his communication with the terrorist. For a moment he turned on the computer but quickly turned it off. It was to test Scott's reaction.

"You mentioned having another computer?"

"Actually, not yet – we're looking," Scott said.

"If you need us ..."

"We will."

David had quickly put a tracking device on their car; he needed to know where they were going and who they had connections to. He solicited Ivan's help who was now working full time on the Army Cyber Protection Team. He would now hack into Scott's computer retrieving any email sent or received. Ads for radicalization appeared on two websites.

Daniels, who had helped David on occasion, a friend, offered his help when asked, with surveillance, taking photos of Scott as well as Mindy, meeting with anyone day or night. David would pretend to inadvertently run into him in a bar; he would discuss what he could do teaching people at the gun range with newer weapons.

"This country," a very drunk Scott said as he found David to be a good listener, "is lacking leadership … and legally we can have and carry concealed handguns and buy any gun for that matter." His speech was more of rambling about his discontent with everything.

"I agree with you … lousy leadership … they should all be thrown out."

"What kind of guns, the newer ones?" He looked at David.

"The illegal kind; a newer assault rifle. I bet you've never heard of two of these and I can show you how to use them at a private gun range not far from here."

"You're on … tell me when."

That evening Scott was on the internet, so was Ivan. Daniels and David met with him.

"What terrorist group is he courting?" Daniels asked.

"It looks like someone here in California with a Nibus affiliation, who recruited him … it also mentions terminating someone named Mindy, before making his move."

"His move where?" Daniels questioned Mindy's safety.

"It seems like he intends to carry out something here in California. I believe he's a 'lone wolf' … easy to manipulate, a grudge against anyone or a specific target, I don't know," David said. "Keep monitoring the communication between the two recording everything. I'm also wearing a watch that will record my conversations with him wherever we are."

"He'll probably continue to connect with you because you'll listen to him and can get your hands on what he needs, weapons. He's white, a loner, about thirty, no steady job, needs a cause … I would say he'll go for soft targets, a school, church, maybe shopping malls; he will also factor in an escape or suicide."

"In talking with his recruiter did he mention pressure cookers or explosives?"

"Not yet; Mindy could possibly be in on it."

"I doubt it … she seems to be linked to him as his cover … disposable when no longer needed."

"A lot of what ifs David."

"If he tries to contact me, call me 24/7 on the alternate cell."

"Copy that," Ivan said.

Two days later David took Scott to a gun range outside of town, no one knew him there, he had weapons in the truck he borrowed. If Scott knew his identity, then he might be killed with one of those guns. Scott was now standing behind him.

"How much?"

"More than you can afford, but I'll loan them to you, show you how to shoot 'em if you tell me who you're gonna kill."

"What gave you the idea that I'm going to kill someone?"

"You did – I can see it in your face."

David began to teach him about each weapon and how to fire each one. Scott didn't reveal who or what target he was aiming for. In the meantime David met with the General and the FBI and local police. Daniels and Ivan attended the meeting as did Kyle.

"I put a tracking device on his car and on his girlfriend's ... Daniels."

"I think, my gut tells me he's going for a school, more glory for himself. I saw him studying, pardon the pun, the children outside in a soccer match – he was writing on a notebook, schedules, I assume, of certain activities outdoors."

"Why kill children?" Ivan couldn't fathom the reasoning for this.

"Easy kill and every one of those parents with a dead child will be in anguish forever and remember him or her."

"So he kills then suicide?"

"A possibility ... we can't allow this to happen," David said.

The police and FBI were making suggestions as well as listening to David and those helping him, particularly to surveillance and the on-line rantings and email.

"I have some pictures I pulled up from a camera across the street from a church five miles away; three hours ago Scott was there sitting on a bench across the street taking notes, when services start, probably casualty count ... the church is racially mixed so it's not about race; he could be going for two targets."

From then on an undercover cop would be at the gun range. Kyle was willing to help; he would see how far Mindy was willing to go to reveal anything on Scott's computer, phone calls and what he had verbally expressed about his intentions. Ivan couldn't pull up everything, especially with a new password if one was used; there was.

Two days later she visited Kyle at the store.

"I was in the area and wanted to see you."

"I wanted to see you again, but aren't you married?"

"To him? No way, we're just friends."

"I'm going to lunch … join me?" Kyle said, and I'm not married."

"Yes … sounds good. In an hour both learned a lot about each other.

"I'm going to ask you something very important … don't tell your friend or my life and the lives of others could be in danger."

"I won't tell."

"I believe he's been recruited by a terrorist group, recruited on the internet; a 'lone wolf' so to speak, looking for a cause."

"I'm not believing this – Scott was always a loner, loves weapons … that doesn't make him a bad person."

"No, it doesn't … it's what he does with the weapons or is intending to do with them. You brought in his computer and gave me the password for some reason and I believe you know the truth and wanted to tell someone, me. I did use the password … he's planning to kill, maybe even you, I replaced his hard drive with an older part, he won't know."

"He mentions doing terrible things; mysterious phone calls, trips to the gun range, one with your employee David. Should we alert the police?"

"David's ok … he's not into murder." Kyle didn't reveal David's role in this.

"So now what?"

"Try to find out what he's doing, listen in on conversations, check his computer … we need to know who he's been in contact with. Be careful. I'd like to get to know you."

She smiled. "I have a photographic memory, I don't have to write things down, so he won't find a paper trail to what I know."

"I'm impressed, and I hope I'm wrong and he's a good guy after all."

For the next few weeks David disclosed information to the General and the police. Everyone on the case helped to stop a possible attack or attacks by a lone wolf terrorist ending in a massacre.

Mindy was able to garner information. Scott had revealed certain feelings about wanting to change things; he had mixed feelings about Mindy, thinking he loved her but she was a liability believing she knew his secret – intentions of murdering soft targets. The computer they shared revealed his plan; when he questioned her about initially giving her his password, she denied it. Ivan, with Mindy's help, discovered the new password.

"I'm not called the dizzy blond for nothing ... I don't know it; you never gave it to me, but if you don't believe me ..."

Scott did believe her and for now he needed her; he pretended to be job hunting as he continued to survey both possible targets. He confided in David that he had bought a 45 caliber Glock pistol and asked his help in becoming proficient with it as with the other guns; they met the next afternoon. The FBI agent was also there working as assistant manager.

"So Mindy doesn't appreciate guns," David said to get a response about her.

"No, never cared for them."

"Before you do whatever you're going to do, is it worth it?"

"I have a cause now, something I believe in ... so yes."

They were there for two hours as David worked with him.

When Scott arrived home Mindy was in the shower. He hid the pistol and checked his computer; he found evidence that she had checked his messages. He now knew she had his password. He entered the shower and made love to her; he didn't mention her deception.

"I think I have a job," he told her, "starts tomorrow."

"I'm excited for you ... what is it?"

"I'm going to kill as many people as I can at a nearby church then move to a school five miles from that target and kill again ... all soft targets, then when I escape I'll come for you."

She was startled, "Please don't joke that way, it's not funny."

"I am a recruit to terrorism. I've been reborn; if I can't join the terrorist movements overseas, then I will here."

"Are you going to kill me as well? I can't go with you, not anywhere."

"I don't want you to reveal my secrets … you're pretty close to that Kyle aren't you? Maybe I'll pay him a visit."

He got up from the table after they drank their wine.

"I feel dizzy … what have you done?"

"This will knock you out for several hours." He tied her to a chair strapped with explosives. "When they try to rescue you, the apartment will be incinerated and this will be my way of escape." He began packing his truck and trailer never to return again. There was a hidden camera and microphone installed two weeks earlier in the apartment; the electronics shop gave Mindy instructions on doing this for her safety and evidence. Scott never suspected – no one had come to the house to install the devices.

"Things just got a lot more complicated," Ivan said. "He plans to kill her."

"Agents are stationed in the church as members, also at the school," the agent in charge told them.

"Let's work on getting her out of the apartment," Kyle said.

"Bomb experts are on their way," another agent told them.

Scott made one phone call; it was traced to his recruiter, then he headed for the church and parked some distance away, armed with two pistols and a rifle with several magazines tucked under his jacket. He was welcomed and sat in the middle of the congregation – no one knew except the preacher and two church security guards that worked regularly there, looking to stop vandals. More security, plain clothes and armed, were there seated along with the congregation to stop a massacre. David was there and out of sight, Scott was high on a banned substance, Captagon.

An hour passed as everyone joined in prayer on kneelers; Scott stood up, drew his pistol and was about to fire when he heard someone say, "Everyone be seated; this man in the black jacket has mental problems." It was David who stepped out into the isle. The agents drew their guns.

"Everyone be quiet," the preacher said, "listen."

Scott knew he had been found out and that he wouldn't be leaving alive. He was wearing a vest laced with TATP explosive to commit suicide.

"Drop the gun," one of the agents said prepared to kill him.

"Don't harm these people, they've done nothing to harm you …"

"You lied to me David, are you a policeman?"

"Just someone trying to keep you from a mistake that would haunt you the rest of your life … by the way I'm Army not a cop."

Just then Mindy walked in the front door.

"I left you home strapped with C-4." He was startled at seeing her. The congregation gasped.

"Was I collateral damage?" She looked at Scott in disbelief.

"Drop your weapon," the agent said again.

The preacher then spoke, "Put down your weapon and live … don't waste your life and the lives of innocent people."

Several members of the congregation began to sing a familiar hymn. Scott was unprepared for this. He did finally surrender and was taken away. David returned with Kyle and Mindy to the police station.

"What will happen to him?" she asked an agent.

"He will face multiple charges … terrorism, but not murder; he'll be incarcerated receiving therapy, how long we don't know."

Later, Mindy began a new life with Kyle.

Adrian discussed the dangers that he faced stopping both a terrorist and saving lives.

"There were several who deserved credit for the outcome. I know you were there to help us, but as you pointed out, each time you do, it brings us closer to annihilation – we can't govern ourselves according to the Vegan Council; is that about right?"

"Unfortunately yes."

A few moments later, "I could have replied to Carlile's letter and taken him up on his offer."

Carlile had written David a letter years later which he read to Adrian. It was a compelling argument to join him aboard the Explorer traveling in the Arctic seas surrounding Copenhagen, catching and doing research on sharks living from 272 years old to the one that lived to be 512. The cold and the deep played a role in this; they were carnivorous, around 16-feet long, the oldest vertebrate animals. The researchers used radiocarbon dating technics on the lens of the sharks eyes. "Sounds like we should have gone."

"And my reply was, sounds like someone needs to reconsider and decline the invitation or end up as another of Carlile's trophies."

David laughed.

Ana fixed dinner, she heard the conversation and was determined to lighten the mood; she brought home one of David's favorite movies, 'Forbidden Planet' and a favorite dessert for Adrian. The children were playing … they grew as normal children but had begun learning several subjects at once; genius level. David knew Adrian hadn't enhanced their minds, not purposely.

"Possibly from the use of the machine to enhance your I.Q. … it's just a guess."

~David's Journal~

As they watched HNN, there was news from all over the world – still the most informative news network for 30 years. Lifting the Iran sanctions, which only held for five years, due to Iran breaking the agreement and keeping billions handed to them, was a total disaster. Many of their missiles had targeted several nations including America while helping to fund terrorism within. America was rebuilding as it fought back; it did striking Iran and Russia. Russia had a new premier who was even more aggressive than Vladimir Putin. The Ukraine now totally belonged to Russia along with Syria and areas of Turkey.

Weapons, nicknamed 'Star Wars', were orbiting above, carrying missiles for possibly a final showdown. Armed drones were still popular. David and Ana's eldest children worked on scientific advances from medicines to strides leading to colonizing Mars and beyond. Their youngest concentrated on preserving the environment and harnessing the energy of black holes.

CHAPTER THREE

~David's Journal~

Five years had passed:

David and Ana's family had matured considerably; the world hadn't. Wars were defeating the efforts of peace as the Think Tank and others in several countries, started by David and Adrian, were facing an uncertain future. Adrian had stopped the aging process for both David and Ana, a gift, but there was a purpose in that gift; he hadn't yet revealed what.

David continued to plan missions as analyst and advisor; he had accompanied other American diplomats, even Adrian, to observe what was happening around the world. Terrorist groups were in charge of certain areas of several countries; things had to change.

Both Adrian and David still taught at the University; David hadn't been deployed to do the actual fighting on the battlefield, but was there with the troops to strategize as the fighting continued.

"How are your people with the fighting still continuing?" David asked him.

"The future was handed back to you. Earth's future is still hanging in the balance. When you visited Vega, there were books dedicated to certain species that had ceased to exist over eons of time; they either destroyed themselves by wars or were obliterated by our kind to stop the spread of their wars as they reached out into the universe to find new conquests. Earth was one of these books ... incomplete. I was told I could assist in the evolution of mankind, but not to hammer humanity into a mold forged by us ... by me. Everytime I helped you, your men, Ana, I changed that. Vegans see that as a violation of the agreement we made with them – I couldn't allow you to die, and now, I know they will come."

David just sat, silent for a few moments. "When?"

"I haven't been told... If I were to reveal who I am, perhaps addressing the UN..."

"In my opinion, it could cause a backlash, causing panic."

"Then we could wait until they are coming... and save as many as possible."

"Out of twelve billion on the Earth... is this why you gave Ana and me this gift, stopping the aging process, to procreate somewhere?"

"Yes... I had a plan to save you and your family if this should happen... a gift... say Carlile Ironstone did something to all of us, or not."

"And your future?"

"Uncertain."

"We have to stop this from happening somehow."

Four years passed: Wars followed. Everyone took notice of the ageless couple. David had confided in Ana, everything.

"Adrian is taking a big risk in this if he reveals who he is to a nervous world. He took a probe into space, I was with him; the probe was undetected as he placed it in orbit around the moon to detect anything abnormal; it remains invisible like the one around the sun. Only a matter of time, he said. 'Eyes in the sky.'"

Mars was colonized in certain areas as well as Europa; how would Adrian get the word out?

David was given more time in the machine, boosting his IQ in anticipation of the Vegan destruction of Earth.

Two years passed: New forms of warfare had been developed.

"There has been a war, of sorts, on Vega; the Council, even my Council seat, has been disbanded. They are coming to take your world. A project called the ARK is now being initiated. Those of us who were on the Council are bringing their largest ships to take a million Earthlings several thousand light-years from here to a suitable planet. I delayed telling you until a planet was found; we found it several years ago it's larger than Earth. We, the others, working toward saving humanity, have been terra forming it with plant and animal life from both Earth and Vega. The atmosphere is about the same as here. It's in a system of twenty planets orbiting a yellow sun in the constellation of Orion. I took the liberty of naming it Orion's Belt, after your Unit."

"How do we choose who's going and are those including yourself?"

"I don't know. We are searching for a planet for ourselves. Vegans have a creed not to kill other Vegans unless in extreme circumstances, but they can do great harm especially in this case… banishment for instance."

"You and the Council have been striving to save mankind, why not share our world; would there be that possibility even though the planet is geared for human life – you survived here?"

"We are first to decide who will go and how to go about it. Forming a Committee of many countries and revealing myself to them as extraterrestrial might begin the process."

"We would need a colossal computer to store the data of communication devices, satellites, medical needs, literary matter, history and much more."

"Earth has one … the Phoenix; one of my implanted students, Dr. Griffo, is still in charge of it, growing by the minute; he has exceeded my expectations."

"Is anyone else ageless … we need those to remain with us not only from the Think Tanks; my men? Who is eligible, who isn't?"

"The new atmosphere can do much to improve human life. As for who is eligible, that's for us to discuss with the Committee representing Earth's future. Terrorists will not be going … and even then, mankind will always be at war. A fresh start on your new world should slow things down to a crawl as new nations are born and boundaries are established. Weapons of warfare won't be carried to the new world although they'll be developed."

"Seven months," David told Ana; "those with impairments will also be allowed to go – though the healthy will be given priority."

"Our family?"

"We're going, the children are going, our future grandchildren … one big happy family." David was uneasy about an uncertain future.

"David, it's our only hope … we'll all have this new chance," Ana said.

His serious demeanor turned into a smile, he hugged her … "No taxes."

Adrian summoned all students, former and present, and those members of the Think Tank to attend a class that he and David would teach at the University on the constellation Orion's Belt. Neither the students nor the Think Tank were aware of Earth's impending destruction.

"For each student, mine and yours, this will be an extra credit for raising a previous grade, if needed, by one letter, and learning about Earth's new home."

"How long to prepare them for the exam and how long for us to teach the course?"

"Two weeks."

"Make it three … Thomas is a slow learner; he has the makings of an astronomer – his autism is challenging."

Adrian listened, "Three then."

"This will determine several things."

David had less time learning the material. Adrian insisted that he learn it in one evening in the machine. Their teaching methods were similar. David feared that the students with lower grades would be disqualified and he couldn't protect them. Adrian belayed his fears, that the grades wouldn't have an effect on who would be going and that every one of them would be given a fair chance.

The students and those of the Think Tank who wouldn't receive a grade, if already graduated, were questioning why this course was added.

Adrian replied, "To broaden your knowledge of the unknown."

"So let's get on it," David replied. The lecture began.

"Orion's Belt is made up of three main stars and has a large supergiant star 800 lightyears away. Zeta Orionis or Alnitak is a triple system of two blue supergiant stars of spectral type 09 and a smaller blue-white giant star of type B0111.

Epsilon Orionis or Alnilam is a blue-white supergiant star of spectral type B0 LAB. It is 1,300 lightyears from Earth.

Delta Orionis or Mintaka is a binary system of a bright blue giant star of spectral type 0.5111 and a blue-white star of type B2V. It is approximately 900-light-years from Earth.

Alnilam, Mitaka, and Alnitak form the belt.

The Orion Nebula is dust, hydrogen, and helium and other ionized gases. Pi-3 Orionis is considered a possible location for Earth size planets. Orion's Belt points to a star, Sirius, in the Canis Major Constellation. The Spitzer Space Centauri Dreams Telescope has found 2,300 planet forming disks in the Orion Cloud Complex, a star-forming region some 1,450 lightyears from Earth. 60-70% of the stars in the Orion Complex have disks. Protoplanetary disks are in Orion."

Three weeks later after the classes were taught and the tests were given, Adrian took his ship, still submerged in the Pacific for several years under hundreds of feet of silt and rock, into the upper atmosphere where it remained stationary as he contacted the entire world in every language with the words, "Eminent danger."

No one took the idea of an extraterrestrial seriously and thought he was another crazy, trying to recruit pseudo-religious followers or that perhaps he was a terrorist of some sort; however, they couldn't explain the spaceship. David, along with several members of the Think Tank, revealed what Adrian was doing to save mankind.

Finally believed, that the technology of the spaceship was alien, the American military tried to take it, to confiscate it by force ... Adrian quickly shut them down forcing them to see the big picture, "Destruction on an unprecedented scale."

In the weeks that followed, Adrian met with world leaders at the United Nations. David went with security and three from the Think Tank to every meeting wherever he could encourage those who would listen and prepare. Several government officials, the president and military questioned how many would go and when; it would be by lottery.

"Several billion live on this planet, one million will be taken, the chosen will only know the day they are taken, the others will remain asleep as all life will be destroyed; they will be unaware. Everyone is to be packed, as you humans say, important files, papers, records of health, abilities and will be dressed in a uniform fitting for travel.

These uniforms will be distributed at centers throughout the world, aiding in a stasis mode of travel. Those going will be beamed aboard twenty ships including mine. The planet we have selected for you will sustain life. Similar to Earth, it's much larger. We have been terra forming to produce crops and vegetation; animal species are native to our world but it is suggested that seeds, and species of cloned embryos be brought aboard, this would include marine life. Procreation will be at your discretion.

"But why are we being singled out?" An African dictator asked.

"Your destruction was eminent the moment you first invented weapons. We Vegans bought you more time but wars continued and now time has run out. Those on my world, who will eradicate mankind, have the deciding vote and will try to stop us from saving anyone. Your civilization isn't the first to be annihilated, to be contained from spreading war to the universe in faster ships, reaching out."

Weeks passed; astronomers began studying the Orion Constellation; the planet was found … they questioned the atmosphere that would sustain mankind.

Discussions among the Think Tanks, worldwide, included ways of growing several things in the new climate including animal sources. New fuels, water sources, education, and ways of preventing wars were discussed.

"They still fight, we still fight Oaloff; we kill to save lives and broker peace," David said.

"And many lives have been spared in the process … by the way you and Ana haven't aged; I'm envious."

"I don't know … sometimes I would have preferred to age or die on the battlefield; band of brothers, but then there was Ana."

"No Ana, no kids, what you would have missed, and us."

"Speaking of us, you guys, wives, kids are going … and Charlotte."

"If this is a lottery and you already know…"

"It's not totally a lottery, don't tell anyone. I told Adrian, all of us or none of us. Marry Charlotte, you love her, before we leave."

"Is there some reason you're rushing this? It's been twenty years, I know."

"Husbands, wives, and children will be put in stasis together."

They did marry the next evening; the others that David had commanded were married and had extended families.

Cecily and Grant weren't leaving, as his health had deteriorated; this was devastating news.

Most in the military believed the message as did the representatives at the United Nations and prepared; the no weapons rule would be strictly adhered to.

"It puts everyone on an equal footing," the President said in a televised message, "I can only hope that I, and the leaders around the world, can come together and forge a treaty of peace; a new day, a new world, a new chance."

Everyone would wear a stasis uniform while they slept the last night on Earth.

The twenty ships arrived and remained in orbit. There were documents from all over the world transferred into the Phoenix computer which was placed aboard one of the larger ships. Adrian's ship while large in size, would carry David, Ana, his family, his men, their families and dignitaries, from several countries, military, medical, conservationists, scientists, biologists, and governing officials capable of restructuring a nation and its economy and infrastructure. Others from around the world were to be taken aboard reflecting other capabilities.

"Tomorrow," Adrian told him a month later, take time for goodbyes. "Everyone will sleep for several months aboard ship; as I said, those who remain won't be aware … no pain, no suffering."

Mike was brought back to America with Mayla and their two children. He had helped in defeating several key terrorists over eight years, leaking information as to where they were hiding – their funding sources, moves.

Mayla loved and respected him putting her own life in danger … she was no longer a terrorist and became a part of David's family leaving for a new existence on another world. David and Ana were notified.

As he and David became reacquainted, there were hugs and tears. Cecily and Grant had seen Mike and the extended family briefly.

"They've definitely got to have beer where we're going. The years went by so quickly."

"I'm proud of you Mike, all you've accomplished … and your family."

"And you Uncle … I wanted to be like you … now you and Ana haven't aged, what's up? And having two sets of triplets – they are my family."

"I'll tell you sometime and about how Adrian and I forged a friendship that saved both our lives; don't forget, put the suits on tonight."

David and Ana had made phone calls to relatives and friends; they took other memorabilia as they would never see Earth again. She left for a few moments as David contemplated leaving forever. He entered his study and took a Menorah, then entered her study, found a bible, looked at it and put it in his jacket pocket hoping if he wore the jacket it might be beamed aboard as well. Ana was now standing behind him. "He needs this journey, a new chance, a new world … we all need this new chance. He's filled with emotional scars from what he had to do when he joined Nibus; he has kept it well hidden. These things take time as you know."

She touched his shoulder, "Time to sleep … no television."

He turned to her, kissing her passionately, "Well, I think we'll get by without it." They slept. She didn't mention the jacket.

Earth was destroyed after the ships departed with their precious cargo. A Vegan faction, sent to destroy, knew the rescue would occur, not exactly when or where they were going; their ships were faster and were in pursuit not allowing humanity to pollute the order of things bringing war and devastation wherever they went.

Earlier David had asked, "Can a human life become important to those Vegans bent on destroying us … be transformed into a Vegan lifeform?"

"I don't see how … what made you ask?"

"Just possibilities; if they believed that we were a type of Vegan, say a hybrid, would this make us important, if we shared some of the characteristics?"

Adrian reflected on David's question as he discussed this with Vegan doctors and scientists travelling with them; they didn't have much time.

Both David and Ana were removed from stasis and told the risks involved.

"Is there some way of creating a Vegan signature for each one of us?"

"Counselor Mafusa," Adrian was called this out of respect, "it might be possible," a Vegan scientist said.

"We volunteer," David said.

In an hour they experienced a transformation while looking as they did before; they watched the destruction of Earth on a screen, the others remained in stasis, unaware.

"They are pursuing us, the destruction of Earth is complete, five ships of enormous power; we are targets as well, as we'll fight to protect the human race... what's left of it." Adrian was frustrated.

"Do we stay awake?"

"For the time being."

Two weeks into the journey, five Vegan ships arrived; five high ranking officials and their security beamed aboard.

"Counselor Mafusa," the official in charge was respectful, "we are offering you your lives, no banishment, to release the humans to us, and to be on the Council as a respected member."

"Just not head of the Council and handing them over means annihilation."

"No, I have assumed that position ... yes, we will exterminate the remnant."

"I want to present two humans, Vegan hybrids, David and his mate, Ana; they have agreed to live their lives under our protection as have the remnant of humanity we are bringing to a new world; no weapons, just technology, the sciences, education, pursuing conservation and the like."

"Let me talk to them." The new Head of Council seemed surprised by this revelation.

Adrian agrees, "Do no harm."

"I met you David, several Earth years ago on Vega."

"Good to meet you again Sir ... this is Ana, my mate."

He examined both as he held both their hands and read their minds.

They briefly changed form, appearing Vegan, then back again.

"I'm impressed." He looked at Adrian. "So one million is all you could save and you're literally creating new lifeforms dedicated to pursuing peace."

"Yes, Counselor."

"There might be a way around all of this. We have always been interested in new lifeforms, but never has one been created by our kind."

David and Ana were allowed to attend a meeting of the Council aboard ship.

"It has been decided, Counselor Mafusa, to allow you to continue your research on the planet you call Orion's Belt. We will permit this only if Vegan supervision is in force there ... not a dictatorship, but guiding these Vegan hybrids into a peaceful existence as they learn our ways. You and those who risked everything will be regarded highly on our world. We'll be watching; a seat on the Council is yours upon your return."

Both Adrian and the Head of Council gave their traditional goodbyes.

"David, you and Ana will return to stasis. He was visibly impressed by you both; the others will be changed as well ... it was a good suggestion, the human race will survive. Two years will pass before we reach home world."

"Are we Vegan?"

"A small fraction of DNA was given; you are still human with a Vegan signature. Only when needed or desired will you temporarily change form."

"You and your fellow Vegans risked everything ... we will share this planet."

"We will remain with the human race for as long as we're needed; there are others on Orion's Belt preparing for our arrival." Adrian smiled.

Two years later: The ships arrived, the memories of Earth would always be etched in their minds, but they faced a certain future of hope and security and friendships as they set foot on a new world, terraformed and transformed as cities had been built in traditional Vegan and human habitats. Traditional internet and other forms of communication were established.

"A beginning," Adrian said, "a large school when it's finished ... as I continue to teach ... that could use a professor I know and TA ... the possibilities are endless. That observatory is the largest ever seen; new modes of travel, structures, offices, homes visiting other star systems."

"What of war, as we will be free?"

"Yes, everyone will be free, even as new countries are declared and boundaries set ... there will be wars; education will be our best tool and a penalty, a warning then banishment to somewhere off world."

"The future then isn't set."

"Let's go study our surroundings and prepare for the future."

The future isn't set
~There are times for war and times for peace~

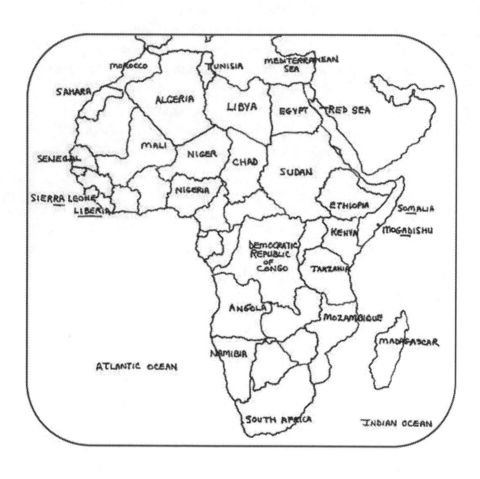

California

EUREKA

• CHICO
CALAVERAS BIG TREES PARK
YOSEMITE NATIONAL PARK

SACRAMENTO

SAN FRANCISCO

PACIFIC OCEAN

• SAN JOSE

National Veterans
Cemetary

LOS ANGELES

Orange County
Los Alamitos Joint
Forces Training Base

LONG-
BEACH

SAN DIEGO

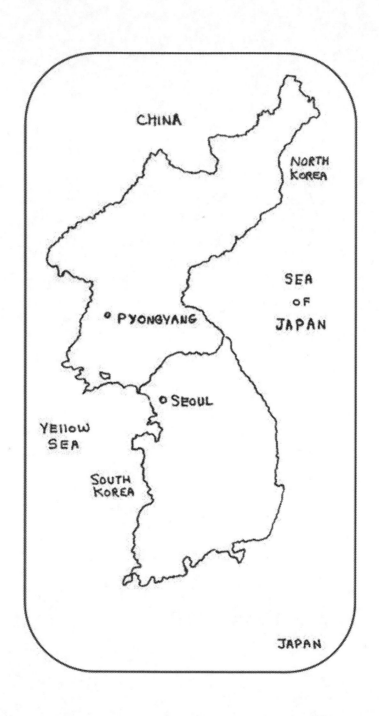

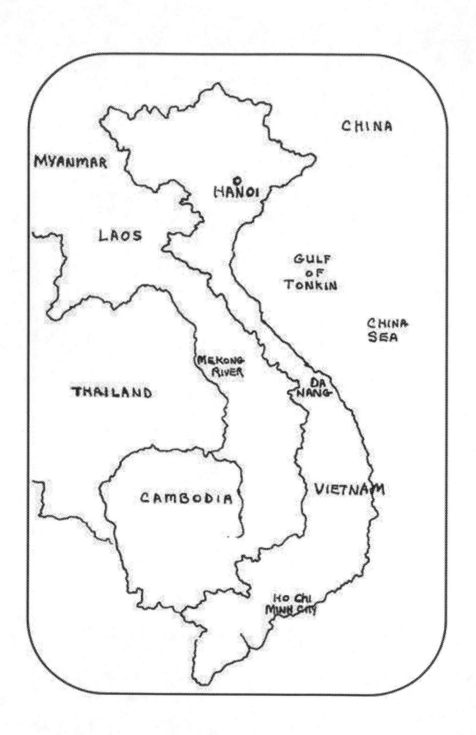

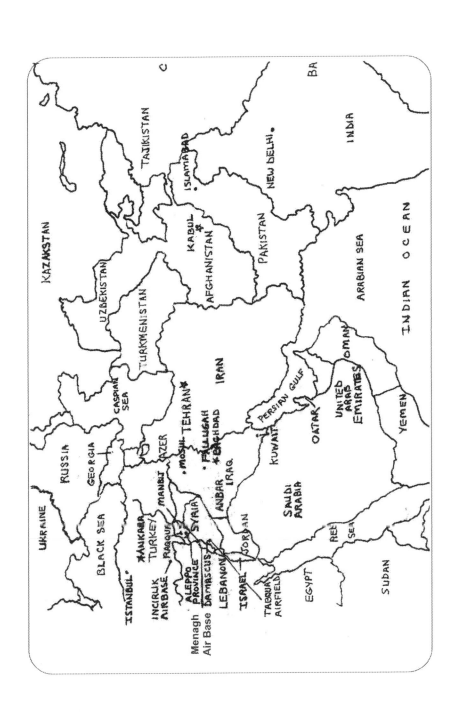

Printed in the United States
By Bookmasters